BBC

DOCTOR WHO

BBC CHILDREN'S BOOKS

UK | USA | Canada | Ireland | Australia
India | New Zealand | South Africa

BBC Children's Books are published by Puffin Books,
part of the Penguin Random House group of companies
whose addresses can be found at global.penguinrandomhouse.com.

www.penguin.co.uk   www.puffin.co.uk   www.ladybird.co.uk

First published 2016
001

Written by Justin Richards
Copyright © BBC Worldwide Limited, 2016

BBC, DOCTOR WHO (word marks, logos and devices),
TARDIS, DALEKS, CYBERMAN and K-9 (word marks and devices) are
trademarks of the British Broadcasting Corporation and are used under licence.
BBC logo © BBC, 1996. Doctor Who logo © BBC, 2009

Printed in Great Britain by Clays Ltd, St Ives plc

A CIP catalogue record for this book is available from the British Library

ISBN: 978–1–405–92872–4

All correspondence to:
BBC Children's Books
Penguin Random House Children's
80 Strand, London, WC2R 0RL

BBC DOCTOR WHO

THE AMERICAN ADVENTURES

PUFFIN

CONTENTS

ALL THAT GLITTERS

Most days, Josh Langham found nothing at all. But occasionally – just occasionally – he would catch a glimpse of something glittering in his pan, as he sifted through the mud. Over the past few months, Josh had found a fair few nuggets of gold in the dirt and sand of the Sacramento River. Some were quite big. They hadn't made him rich – not by a long way – but it was enough to live on at least.

As Josh worked away under the intense heat of the California sun, he daydreamed that today would be the day he'd find the one huge, gleaming piece of gold ore that would change his life forever. He wouldn't have to work another day in this sun again, and would be able to have anything his heart desired.

After another sieve of nothing but gravel, Josh paused for a moment. He wouldn't let disappointment get to him – not today. He pushed his wide-brimmed hat back from his forehead and ran a hand across it, wiping away the sweat, before digging his pan into the mud again.

As he picked through yet another batch of grey river stones and sand, Josh caught sight of something gleaming. The familiar feeling of sudden excitement rose rapidly, and his heart rate quickened . . . only to fall again as more of the object was revealed and he saw that it was not gold but silver.

Josh picked the object out of the mud. Now that he peered closer, he saw that it didn't even appear to be real silver, but some sort of metal. It looked artificial, machined somehow. It was roughly cylindrical, about the size of his thumb, but ridged with a pattern of lines and indentations. He rinsed the strange object in the flowing water of the river, then returned to the riverbank to examine it more closely.

Definitely man-made, Josh decided. There was no way it could be a natural object.

He wondered what its purpose might be. Was it a container with something inside – something valuable, perhaps? If so, the object had been perfectly sealed; Josh couldn't see a join anywhere on it.

He held the object up, letting its reflective surface glint in the sunlight. It was certainly intriguing, but Josh couldn't help but dwell on the *real* question: was it valuable?

As Josh stared at the object's metallic surface, he felt his eyes begin to close, his eyelids suddenly as heavy as he had ever felt them. It was as if he was falling asleep – but that was crazy. He'd slept well last night, and had only been up for a couple of hours. He shouldn't be feeling tired, and, even if he was, the burning heat was enough to keep him awake.

Even so, a mist of blackness slowly enveloped Josh's consciousness and a few moments later he toppled sideways. He lay motionless, still gripping the strange object and staring up at the bright sun. But, even though his eyes were wide open, he saw nothing.

The sun was setting and it was getting dark by the time Josh finally stirred.

Slowly, he sat up, then he got to his feet. He slipped the small, metal object into the pocket of his battered jacket. Then, for several minutes, he stood completely still on the bank of the river, staring off into the distance as the light faded around him.

At last he moved. He started to walk, heading for the nearest town at an urgent pace, as if there was something he suddenly needed to do.

The town was several miles away, and it took Josh a couple of hours to reach it.

When he got within sight, he stopped and waited, staring across the dusty plain to where the dark silhouettes of the buildings thrust up into the sky, warm lights flickering in their windows.

He waited for the last of the lights to be extinguished before he continued, walking slowly and deliberately until he reached the barn where Jesse Hayward the blacksmith worked. It was locked up for the night.

Josh spent a few minutes examining the lock. He had no idea how to pick a lock – he'd never had any reason to before – so he put his shoulder to the side door and smashed it open.

He strode into the barn.

As he searched for what he needed, there wasn't even a hint of remorse – or any other emotion – on his face. He had other places he needed to visit and other items to collect, but, with its plentiful supply of metal, this barn would make an excellent starting point.

Jesse Hayward lived above the barn where he did his work. He'd had a long day. It was good to be busy, but it meant he never got to bed before midnight. And now, for some reason, he couldn't settle.

He was finally just drifting off to sleep when he heard the sound of splintering wood.

At once he was wide awake. Another crash came from what he now realised was the door of the barn. Without a second thought, Jesse leapt out of bed. He grabbed his coat from a hook by the door and ran down the stairs.

As he got closer to his workshop, he could hear someone moving about inside. Who on earth would be in there, at this time of night? Jesse slowed his pace and crept carefully down the last of the stairs, not wanting to alert whoever had broken in.

At the bottom of the stairs, Jesse paused, crouched in the darkness. The barn was pitch black. He cursed himself for not bringing a lamp – but then the clouds drifted away from the moon, and a shaft of moonlight fell through the window.

Jesse could see a man moving methodically around the barn. He had his back to Jesse, and he seemed to be gathering together a pile of metal. Some of it was scrap, some of it bits and pieces that Jesse had been machining and shaping for specific clients.

Before Jesse could call out to the man, he turned round.

Jesse recognised him at once. It was Josh Langham, one of the prospectors. What did he think he was doing, breaking in here in the middle of the night?

Josh stared at Jesse for a moment, then hurled himself straight at the blacksmith, grabbing Jesse by the shoulders and throwing him backwards. Jesse crashed into the bottom of the stairs, his legs crumpling and his head cracking on one of the wooden steps. He tried to get up, but felt himself losing consciousness.

His last thought before he passed out completely was that the black mist now clouding his vision was as dark as Josh's eyes had been. He'd never seen anything like it before – a human with eyes that were completely and utterly black . . .

It was daylight when Jesse Hayward's eyes opened again and his vision slowly cleared.

His head was throbbing, and he was lying on his bed, but he couldn't remember how he'd got there. Stranger still, there was a man he didn't recognise bending over him. The man had a face that somehow seemed both stern and friendly at the same time, with pronounced, frowning eyebrows and greying hair.

The man straightened up and nodded. 'OK. You'll be fine now,' he said, already striding away from the bed and towards the stairs.

Jesse struggled to sit up. 'Who are you?' he said, his words slightly slurred.

The man stopped and turned back to the bed. 'I'm the Doctor,' he said. 'Not technically a medical doctor, but I can assure you there's no lasting damage done. You'll probably have a headache for a while, nothing more.' Then, apparently deciding to stay put for a little longer, he sat down in a nearby chair. 'You want to tell me what happened?'

'Someone broke into my barn,' Jesse said. Events were rather misty in his memory. He tried hard to remember exactly what had happened. 'They were gathering metal. All sorts of scrap, things I'd been working on . . .'

'Interesting,' the Doctor said, nodding. 'And you disturbed them, I assume?'

Jesse nodded, and wished he hadn't as his head throbbed more severely. 'I heard them smash open the door and went to look . . .' His voice trailed off as he remembered more. 'It was Josh!' he exclaimed. 'The prospector, Josh Langham! But −' he frowned − 'that's not like Josh at all. Why would he do such a thing?' he asked quietly.

The Doctor shrugged. 'I have no idea. Anything else you can remember?'

Jesse nodded, slowly and carefully this time. 'His eyes.'

'What about them?'

'There was something odd about them,' Jesse said, trying to remember. Then it came to him – a sudden recollection, a vision of Josh's face looming close to his own as he pushed Jesse back. 'His eyes were completely black.'

'Really?' The Doctor frowned. 'That doesn't sound good. That doesn't sound good at all.'

'So what are we going to do?' Jesse asked. 'About Josh, I mean. Is he still in town?'

The Doctor stood up. 'We're not going to do anything. *You*,' he said severely, pointing at Jesse, 'are going to get some rest. And by tomorrow you'll be all recovered and ready to help me do . . . whatever I decide to do.'

And, with that, the Doctor turned once more and stomped out of the room. Moments later Jesse heard the sound of the broken barn door slamming.

The next morning, after a good night's sleep, Jesse did indeed feel a lot better. His first job, he thought, would be to get the barn door mended and the lock replaced.

Until, that was, he walked downstairs and found the Doctor waiting for him.

'Feeling better?' The Doctor didn't wait for an answer. 'Good, because I need your help. You know this Josh Langham, right?'

Jesse blinked, taken aback by the demanding tone of this stranger who had walked, yet again, uninvited into his home. Looking at the man's steely expression, however, Jesse decided it would probably be best to give him the information he was after.

'Most people know Josh. He comes into town for supplies every now and again.' Jesse shrugged. 'I suppose I know him as well as anyone here does.'

'Good. Come with me.'

The Doctor led Jesse out of the barn and to the saloon. A number of folk from the town were waiting and the Doctor gestured for Jesse to sit with them.

It seemed that Jesse's barn wasn't the only place Josh had broken into. After his encounter with Jesse, Josh seemed to have been scared off; he had taken the metal and left town. But then last night he had come back.

'We don't know for sure it was Josh,' one woman pointed out.

'Be a hell of a coincidence if it wasn't,' someone else growled.

The Doctor nodded. 'The question you should really be asking is *why* he's doing this. You all say it's out of character – seems a bit of an understatement to me.'

Jesse listened, still feeling a little dazed. Josh had also taken wood from the woodyard, and leather from the cobblers. He had broken into the village's general store too, although he had left such a mess there that no one was quite sure what he'd taken.

'What are we going to do about it?' someone demanded.

The Doctor stood up and planted his hands authoritatively on the table. 'It's very simple,' he said. 'We are going to find Josh Langham and ask him what he's up to.'

Jesse rubbed the lump on the back of his head. 'Assuming he's willing to cooperate,' he murmured.

'I suggest we start by looking along the river for his camp,' came a voice from the back of the room.

Jesse turned in surprise. It was Sheriff Harlan; he was standing at the back of the saloon. This Doctor, whoever he was, obviously had some clout if he'd managed to get the sheriff involved. Then again, a crime was a crime – and, by the sound of it, there were several here to be investigated.

So it was agreed: in one hour, they would all meet back outside the saloon with their horses and provisions. It could take all day to find Josh – especially if he didn't want to be found – and they needed to be prepared.

'Do you have a horse?' Jesse asked the Doctor.

'I don't, no,' the Doctor replied. His spiky eyebrows furrowed.

'It's all right,' Jesse grinned. 'You can borrow one of mine. I can only ride one at a time.'

An hour later, Sheriff Harlan led the group from the saloon down the main street and out of the town, the Doctor riding close beside him. While the sheriff was 'officially' leading the way, it was fairly clear – at least to Jesse – that it was really the Doctor who was in charge.

Jesse manoeuvred his horse closer to Dan Burrows, who owned the woodyard. The two had known one another for years and were good friends.

'So do you know who exactly this Doctor is?' Jesse asked.

Dan shook his head. 'Turned up yesterday. Came into the barn just after John Jones and I found you unconscious. We saw the door was smashed in and came to see if everything was all right.'

'Seems to have the sheriff's ear, whoever he is,' Jesse said.

'He does that. Got quite an air of authority about him. He organised me and John to carry you upstairs to your bedroom, then insisted we leave him to wait and see you were all right when you came round.'

'Well, he did do that,' Jesse confirmed. 'Thanks for getting me up to bed. Probably more comfortable than lying on the stairs.'

Dan laughed. 'Probably,' he agreed.

✿

They made their way down to the river first; everyone knew that Josh panned for gold, with some success, in its waters. The trail down into the valley where the river ran was steep and treacherous in places, but the horses managed without too much trouble.

They headed upstream along the bank, away from the town and towards the hills. This seemed the most likely place for Josh to have camped. He would want to be as far upstream as possible in order to find any gold before anyone else spotted it. Also, the further along it ran, the deeper the river became as other streams fed into it. Panning was definitely easier closer to the hills.

Each rider kept a keen lookout for any sign of Josh, but it wasn't until the afternoon that they finally found his campsite.

His tent was pitched close to the river. There were the remains of a campfire, and Josh's pan was propped up against one of the tent's guy ropes. The whole campsite looked as if Josh had just left it a few minutes earlier – except that the fire was cold ashes, and there was no sign of the prospector at all.

The Doctor jumped down from his horse and started to examine everything in detail. The sheriff dismounted too, and soon everyone was helping the Doctor to hunt for clues.

Finally, the Doctor stopped and placed his hands on his hips.

'Josh hasn't been here for a while,' he announced, although everyone else had already come to this same conclusion. 'And he went that way.' He pointed off to the edge of the campsite where there was a gap in the nearby trees.

'How could you possibly know that?' one of the men scoffed.

The Doctor seemed unruffled by the man's derisive tone. 'We didn't pass him on the way here, so he didn't go downstream. He hasn't taken his pan, so he isn't panning for gold. That means he doesn't need to be by the river. And, in any case, upstream from here the riverbank gets very high and steep. I'd guess that this is as far upstream as Josh felt he could sensibly make camp. So that leaves –' the Doctor pointed to the gap in the trees. Then he jogged back to his horse, jumped up into the saddle and continued. 'Plus, you can see there are footprints in the mud. They lead away from the campsite – and they don't come back again!'

'So we follow Josh's footprints,' the sheriff said, nodding.

'As far as we can,' the Doctor agreed. 'After that we'll have to guess where he might be headed. To me, it looks like he was making for the hills.'

They were at the base of the range of hills – the river came down from the hills, which was why it became harder to follow as it wound further upstream.

Jesse wondered what Josh could be doing up in the hills. There was nothing up there, and the terrain was dangerous. The pain in his head began to throb again as he considered whether Josh had actually meant to escape, or whether he had wanted to be followed all along.

As they made their way up into the hills, the ground became drier, rocky and uneven. Before long it was impossible to make out Josh's footprints, and there were no other clues to follow.

'What do you suggest now, Doctor?' Sheriff Harlan asked. The path they were on had become a narrow trail that was difficult for the horses to navigate.

The Doctor looked stern. 'It still appears that Josh was heading up into the hills,' he said at last. 'If you're all still with me, let's carry on.'

'He'll see us coming from miles off if he's anywhere along this path!' Dan hissed to Jesse, and Jesse had to agree – they had no chance of catching Josh off guard.

The horses plodded on, getting slower and slower as the trail got steeper.

Finally, they rounded a corner and the Doctor and the

sheriff pulled abruptly to a halt.

'Well,' Sheriff Harlan said, letting out a low whistle. 'I'll be darned. There he is.'

Past the Doctor and the sheriff, Jesse could see the motionless figure of Josh Langham. He was sitting by the side of the trail and didn't seem at all aware of their presence. If they got any closer, Jesse thought, Josh would certainly see them. Then he'd probably leap to his feet and run for it.

Except he didn't move at all. Only when the Doctor approached him and tapped him gently on the shoulder did Josh slowly look up. There were gasps from everyone – even the most hardened of the town's folk.

Only the Doctor seemed unsurprised, sighing as if this was exactly what he had expected.

Josh's face was pale and expressionless. He stared blankly up at the men on horses close by. But it was his eyes themselves that were the strangest thing. They were exactly as Jesse remembered them from the barn: completely black.

The Doctor whispered into Josh's ear, too quietly for Jesse or anyone else to hear. Then he took something from his pocket. It looked like a metal tube, but when the Doctor held it out towards Josh it made a high-pitched whirring sound and the end lit up with a brilliant blue glow. The light illuminated

Josh's face, and was reflected back perfectly in his mirror-like, glassy black eyes.

Incredibly, as Jesse and the others watched, Josh's expression seemed to clear. The blackness of his eyes slowly faded and drifted away like clouds after a storm, when the sun begins to break through. Finally, Josh blinked and stared round at everyone in surprise.

'Where am I?' he asked, sounding confused, and then a little afraid. 'Why are you all here?'

The Doctor peered intently into Josh's eyes, then slapped him on the shoulder. 'That's more like it!' he said. 'I'm the Doctor. You've had a bit of a funny turn, young Josh. But we're all here to help. Now, what's the last thing you remember?'

Josh slowly shook his head. 'I'm not sure. I . . . I must have been dreaming. I dreamt that I went into town . . . and I took metal from Jesse's barn. And some wood from Dan's woodyard. Other things, too.'

The Doctor nodded encouragingly. 'Good. That's very good. And what did you do with the metal and the wood and the other stuff?'

Josh put a hand to his head, evidently still confused. 'I don't remember. I took it up into the hills, I think.' He gestured on up the trail and frowned as he tried to remember.

'I was building something.'

'What sort of something?' the Doctor asked.

'I have no idea. I'm sorry. I just knew I had to make it.
It was automatic, somehow.'

The Doctor sat down beside Josh, rubbing his forehead
and frowning as if trying to solve a difficult puzzle. 'What's
the last thing you remember before this dream where you
went into town, Josh?' he asked. 'It may not seem significant
to you, but it might be very important.'

Josh stared off into the distance as he tried to recall what
had happened.

'I was panning for gold,' he said at last. 'Down at the
river, where I set up camp. I . . . I found something. Not gold,
but something else. I don't know what it was, but it was made
of metal.'

The Doctor nodded and smiled, as if he'd just had a
hunch confirmed. 'And what did you do with the strange
metal something?'

'I picked it up, and then . . . everything went dark.' Josh
turned to look at the Doctor. Then he frowned. 'Hold on.
I think maybe I put it in my pocket.'

He rummaged through what seemed every pocket in
his coat, before he finally found what he was looking for: the
small metal tube. Josh held it out to the Doctor, who took it

carefully – almost gingerly, Jesse thought – from him.

'Thank you,' the Doctor said, as he examined the metal object. 'Yes,' he went on quietly, 'this would do it.'

'Do what?' Josh asked.

The Doctor just smiled, then stood up. 'Sheriff,' he said. 'I want you and everyone else to take Josh here back to town and make sure he's all right. He'll need rest, but he should be fine after a good sleep.'

The sheriff nodded. 'All right, Doctor. If you think that's best. But what about you? Are you coming back with us?'

'Not just yet,' the Doctor replied. 'There's something I need to sort out first. Shouldn't take long.' He made to start walking away, before he quickly turned back and added, 'Oh, and go easy on Josh. He may have committed a little bit of theft and given Jesse there a nasty bump on the head, but I can assure you it wasn't his fault. And it won't be happening again.'

Then, without waiting for a response, the Doctor started to run uphill along the narrow trail. Jesse quickly grabbed the reins of the horse the Doctor had been riding, before it wandered off.

'Josh can have my horse!' the Doctor called back as he ran. 'A bit of a jog will do me good.'

Jesse was surprised to feel a pang of sadness as he

watched the Doctor jog away. He was quite quick for a man
of his years, both on his feet and in his mind. In fact, there
was something unusual about the Doctor in every aspect,
Jesse thought. Maybe even something a little . . . *otherworldly*.

As he watched the Doctor climb higher into the hills,
Jesse had a strong suspicion that none of them would meet
anyone quite like him ever again.

On his way up the steep path, the Doctor examined the metal
object that Josh had given him. It confirmed what he already
knew: the small metal cylinder was a storage chamber. What
it stored was a sentient mind, which it kept safe over the
course of an extended space voyage – a journey that might
last centuries. At the end of the journey, the mind would be
reunited with its body, which was stored cryogenically or in
some form of stasis; during the journey, however, the mind
would remain active – although confined to the
metal chamber.

The question intriguing the Doctor was: how had it
come to Earth? Perhaps some accident had destroyed an
alien ship, and only this storage chamber had survived, falling
through the atmosphere to land in the Californian hills, where
it had been washed down the river for Josh to find it.

One thing was certain, at least: when Josh had found

it, the mind inside had transferred into his, taking him over. Possessing him.

Which brought the Doctor to his next question: what had the mind made Josh build, exactly? And where was that mind now?

The Doctor continued to ponder these questions as he made his way up the steep path, which seemed to go on forever. He stopped a couple of times to get his breath back. The afternoon sun was beating down, and he began to wish he'd kept the water bottle that had been strapped to his horse.

Eventually, the Doctor rounded a corner and there ahead of him was a dark, gaping opening in the side of the hill. A cave.

It was immediately apparent that this was where Josh had brought the items he had stolen. Pieces of metal and wood were strewn across the ground in front of the cave's mouth.

There was no sign, however, of what it was that Josh had been working on, so the Doctor cautiously ventured inside the cave. As it grew darker, he took out his sonic screwdriver and used it as a torch.

What he saw in the sonic's light was rather disappointing – the cave only went back about thirty feet. The Doctor could see to the back wall, and there was no other way out.

No tunnels leading off or mysterious, dark alcoves where something might be hidden. It was just your average cave, and it was completely empty. Not even a little bit exciting.

Unsure what his next move should be, the Doctor walked back outside.

He put away his sonic screwdriver, and sat down on a large rock close to the mouth of the cave. The view was breathtaking – emerald-green fir trees and immense, sandy plains with the river carving its way between them – but the Doctor was too deep in thought to enjoy it.

The mind that had possessed Josh had wanted him to build something; and, presumably, Josh had done just that. The mind had sent him back down the hill and pretty much abandoned him. For all his blank expression and dark eyes, Josh's own mind had needed only a little coaxing to reassert itself. Whatever had possessed him had all but gone by the time the Doctor and the others found Josh.

If the mind had finished with Josh, that meant that he had already done whatever it had wanted him to do. And all the clues pointed to him having done it here by this cave.

With a sigh, the Doctor stood up and dusted down his velvet jacket. His only option was to continue to hunt until he found something.

As it happened, he didn't have to find it; it found him.

He was making his way round the side of the cave and up a narrow path that led towards the summit of the hill. He was keeping close to the mountain side, as on the other side was a sheer drop. A glance over the edge was all it took for the Doctor to learn that the ground fell away completely; if he slipped, he would fall over fifty feet before his body crashed into the jagged rocks below.

The Doctor heard it before he saw it.

From somewhere close by came a clanking, metallic sound.

The Doctor stopped and listened carefully.

There was the sound again.

The scrape of metal on stone, the Doctor thought. There could be a perfectly normal explanation. Perhaps someone was dragging something heavy and metallic over the hillside close by, as he was sure people often did . . .

As the Doctor turned to try to work out which direction the noise was coming from, a figure rose on the path above and stared down at him. Or, at least, the Doctor assumed it was staring – it was hard to tell.

The figure was made entirely of pieces of metal, lengths of wood and other scrap, all crudely fixed together. The body was built in the rough shape of a man, with two arms and two legs and a great lump that the Doctor imagined was supposed to be a head.

As the figure lumbered down the path, its metal feet scraped against the rocky ground. The Doctor gulped as he noticed several long, sharp blades of metal protruding from its limbs, and the heavy, club-like blocks of wood at the ends of its arms.

'So, *this* is what Josh was doing,' the Doctor said loudly. 'Making you a new body. Can't say it's much of a looker.'

The makeshift figure paused. When it answered, the Doctor didn't so much hear its words as understand instinctively what it was telling him.

Some form of telepathy, he concluded.

The alien's mind was reaching out to his just as it had to Josh – except that it had possessed Josh, while for now it was merely communicating.

The words formed in the Doctor's mind.

You know what I am?

'Well, in general terms,' the Doctor admitted. 'I'm a visitor here myself. I imagine you ended up here by some sort of accident?'

That is correct. My mind survived. Now I have a body again.

'Well, yes,' the Doctor agreed. 'Sort of. It doesn't look too elegant, if you don't mind my saying.'

It is a temporary problem.

'Oh, really?' The Doctor raised his eyebrows. 'I was

going to offer you a ride home, actually. I'm guessing you'll be able to grab a new body there?'

He could sense the alien becoming irritated by his questions.

I cannot go home. The ship I was on was taking me and others into exile. I am a criminal convicted of crimes and facing punishment. I shall make my home here.

The Doctor sighed. 'I'm not entirely sure you'll fit in,' he said.

The figure began to lurch down the path towards him again.

It is not a question of fitting in. This planet seems most suitable. I shall make myself the ruler of the primitive humans that inhabit it. And, later, I shall take whatever body I want.

The figure had almost reached the Doctor now. Suddenly it lashed out with one of its huge arms.

The Doctor ducked just in time, but he felt one of the sharp blades slice through the air right above his head. As he stepped back, his foot slipped on the uneven path and he almost fell. He just managed to regain his balance, then continued to back away, risking a glance behind and hoping he wasn't too close to the edge of the precipice.

Do not think that you can escape from me.

The words echoed inside the Doctor's head.

Once I have disposed of you, I shall return to the town where the human obtained the materials to build this body.

'Oh yes?' the Doctor said, keeping well back. 'And what will you do there?'

I shall make the humans proclaim me as their leader.

'So you're another maniac who wants to rule the world,' the Doctor said. He yawned theatrically, then added, 'Sorry, I'm just a bit bored of the whole megalomaniac thing.'

It is more than that, the voice hissed. *Once the humans are under my control, I shall make them do my will. I shall turn them into an army that I will return to my own world with and use to conquer it.*

'So you think you can control humans?'

Of course. Although, the voice admitted, *your mind seems to resist my power.*

'Yes, sorry about that. Not human, see?' He pointed to his chest and his two hearts, guessing that the telepathic link would allow the alien to understand. 'And I'm also sorry that I can't let you go through with your plan.'

The Doctor heard the alien's laughter inside his head.

You will not be here to stop me, you puny primitive!

The figure lunged forward, both of its huge arms flailing. If either hit the Doctor, the blow would almost certainly be fatal.

But the Doctor just smiled. 'I was hoping you'd do that,'

he murmured as the creature sailed through the air.

The Doctor dropped suddenly to the ground, then surged forward – not away from the flailing mass of wood and metal, but towards it. The Doctor collided with the figure's legs and, shoving with his full weight, swept them out from beneath its huge, heavy body.

With a roar first of anger, then of fear, and so loud it shook the Doctor's brain, the figure toppled forward. The momentum kept it moving – it rolled over the top of the Doctor and across the narrow path. The Doctor got back to his feet just in time to see the figure plunge over the sheer precipice.

The scream in his mind was cut abruptly short as the figure hit the jagged rocks far below. As the Doctor watched, the creature was smashed apart far below, splintered wood and twisted metal flying outwards in an explosive smash, ending scattered far and wide across the ground.

The Doctor stared down at the remains for a few moments. Then he called out, 'Are you still there?'

There was no answer; his mind detected nothing.

The Doctor nodded with satisfaction, and started to make his way slowly back down the path. It would take him a while to reach the town, but when he did he could assure Sheriff Harlan, Jesse, Josh and the others that everything was going to be all right now. Their town, and the future of human civilisation, were both safe.

He wouldn't tell them about the alien, or that its life essence had now dissipated into the atmosphere. To all intents and purposes, whatever life form it had been was now dead and gone.

And soon, the Doctor reflected, *I'll be gone too.* Just a quick word, a hasty goodbye, and he would be on his way.

Though where he would find himself next, he had no idea.

OFF THE
TRAIL

Hattie Seymour was bored. She had been bored for
weeks. Her parents, on the other hand, seemed to
accept the mind-numbing journey without complaint. John
and Elizabeth Seymour were the ones who had decided to
make the trip West, and Hattie still sometimes heard them
whispering excitedly about it, with words like 'opportunity'
and 'a better life' jumping out over and over again.

But Hattie hadn't seen anything better than their old life yet.

When Hattie's parents had first told her they were going
to Oregon to set up a ranch, it had seemed like a good idea.
She had thought it would be a great adventure – heading off
into the untamed wilderness – but now, sitting at the front
of the wagon, all she could see ahead was the next wagon

in the train. And, beyond that, there was nothing but empty, open grassland. There were hardly any hills, and she couldn't remember the last time she had seen a tree.

At night, they would gather the wagons into a circle and make a large fire in the middle. The horses would be tethered nearby, and everyone would sit, eat and chat. Hattie wasn't big on chat. She'd much rather they just got to where they were going. Every day and every night was so much the same she'd lost count. She had no idea how long ago they had left Missouri, and no one in their convoy of wagons seemed to know exactly how long it would take to reach Oregon.

What Hattie didn't know yet, however, was that things were about to become very different.

At the camp that evening, the orange glow of the fire was fading and people had begun to head back to their own wagons, when suddenly the wind picked up. Hattie, who was already in the back of her family's wagon, thought nothing much of it. Out here in the middle of nowhere the wind could be unpredictable.

She wrapped herself in her blankets and called goodnight to her mum and dad. Then she closed her eyes tight, wishing to fall asleep as quickly as possible. There was a chance she might have some interesting dreams – that, at least, would break the monotony.

Hattie had no idea how long she had been asleep when she was jolted awake by her father clambering over her.

'Sorry,' John Seymour said in a gruff whisper. 'Didn't mean to wake you. I need to tie up the back of the wagon. The dust is kicking up something terrible out there. I'm worried for the horses.'

Even with the back of the wagon tied up tight, though, Hattie could still hear the wind howling outside. Once her father was back in his bed, she shuffled out of her blankets and risked a quick peek outside. She could see nothing but dust – not even the next wagon.

She crawled back to her makeshift bed and pulled the blankets back up around her, covering her head. Maybe the noise would be less annoying this way.

Before long, she had fallen fast asleep once more.

When Hattie woke again, the wind had dropped. It still tugged at the covering of the wagon, but nothing like it had done the night before.

At the front of the wagon, both of her parents were still asleep. Hattie could hear her father snoring, so she stayed in bed, staring off into nothing and wondering if today would be different from any of the previous days on the trip. She doubted it.

Hattie didn't realise there was anything wrong until her parents finally woke up. 'Couldn't get to sleep.' Her mother yawned. 'That dust storm was the loudest I've ever heard.'

Hattie smiled, sitting up. 'Don't worry, Mama. I've been awake for a while. No sound from the other wagons yet.'

Everyone else must have slept late too. That was hardly surprising.

It was only when John Seymour opened the back of the wagon, squinting in the bright morning light, that they realised how wrong they were.

They were totally alone. There was no other wagon anywhere in sight. Just their own, and their horses tied up to a large boulder nearby.

'But they wouldn't have just left us!' Elizabeth cried.

John was scratching his head. 'Why wouldn't they just tell us they were leaving?'

But Hattie had noticed something else. Something even stranger. 'There's no sign of the fire,' she said, almost in a whisper.

All three of them climbed out of the wagon and made their way over to where the fire had been burning the night before. Hattie was right. There was nothing. No charred wood, no ashes, nothing at all to suggest there had ever been a fire on this spot.

John looked around, frowning. 'It's just not possible,' he said at last, turning to his family and spreading his arms wide. 'Look around!'

Elizabeth and Hattie both looked. Wasn't it just the same as ever? An empty, barren landscape for as far as the eye could see.

But Hattie's mother's face told her otherwise.

'It's changed,' Elizabeth said quietly. 'Everything's changed.'

John nodded. 'We came through a valley between two hills late yesterday, just before we made camp here. Those hills –' he almost laughed – 'have just . . . gone. There's no sign of them!'

Hattie felt a shiver run through her. 'What are you saying?' she asked. 'That it's not the other wagons that have moved, but *us*?'

'That makes no sense,' her mother said.

'No, it doesn't,' Hattie's father agreed. 'It makes no sense at all, but the facts are the facts. As far as I can see, that's what's happened.'

He sighed, looking up at the sky, his hands on his hips. Hattie knew that look. He was making a plan.

'Well, with the sun up, we can at least work out which

direction we should be heading in. With luck, we'll catch up with the rest of the wagon train before sundown.' He smiled, but it was a smile that didn't reach his eyes.

'How could this possibly happen?' Hattie whispered, more to herself than anyone else.

Neither of her parents had an answer to give her.

With the sun rising in the sky above, John Seymour stuck a long branch into the ground and used the movement of its shadow to find North. From that, he calculated their best course across the open countryside. Before long the family was off again.

After a while, despite the morning's odd events, things started to feel much as they had before. The only thing that had changed on this dull journey was that Hattie was no longer looking at the back of other identical wagons as they travelled – now, it was an endless, blank, dusty landscape.

They reached a valley with steep sides and started through it. For some reason, Hattie began to feel as though they were being watched. It was just a feeling, though – until she looked up at the ridge on one side of them and spotted a quick movement. The sun had glinted for a moment, as though reflecting off something shiny, like a mirror or metal of some sort.

Hattie kept watching, but there was nothing more.

It must be my imagination, she thought. She was so bored that her mind was making things up for fun.

They journeyed on until the light began to fade. John's brow was furrowed with worry, but he tried to hide it. Why had they not seen any sign of the other wagons? How had they got so far apart from the others?

With the sun dipping low on the horizon, the Seymours agreed they should stop for the night. Hattie tethered the horses, while her exhausted parents sorted out blankets and made up their beds. She fell asleep almost at once.

Hattie was woken again by the sound of a terrified cry. Her mother!

She was instantly up, pushing away her blankets and struggling towards the front of the wagon.

'What is it?' she gasped, grabbing her mother by the arm.

'I . . . I don't know,' Elizabeth said. Her eyes were wide and her face pale.

She had been sleeping closest to the front of the wagon, and its canvas cover was open to allow a breeze during the hot night.

'Out there,' she said, pointing to the opening. 'I saw something.'

'What sort of something?' John asked, awake now too and putting his arm round his wife.

But Elizabeth just shook her head. 'I have no idea. It looked –' she took a deep breath – 'like nothing I've ever seen. It shone like metal and it was moving. Going round the wagon.'

The three of them sat in silence for a few moments, listening. But there was no sound from outside.

'I must have imagined it,' Elizabeth said at last, shaking her head. 'Perhaps it was a dream.'

'If there is something out there, I'm going to find it,' John said decisively.

His wife clutched at his arm. 'John, it might not be safe.'

'All the more reason to go and check,' he told her.

'I'll come with you, Dad,' Hattie said. Then, before her father could protest, she added, 'I want to. I'm not afraid. And if there is something out there –' she gulped – 'you're going to need help.'

Her father sighed. 'All right then. Let's take a look together.'

They dressed quickly and clambered out of the wagon. There was a bright moon in the sky, illuminating the landscape, but no sign of anything moving. Even the horses were absolutely still. *Probably asleep*, Hattie thought. It never ceased to amaze her that horses could sleep standing up.

'There's nothing here,' said Hattie, as they peered into the gloom.

'Let's take a quick look around,' John said quietly. 'Just to be sure.'

He led the way cautiously round the wagon, making as little noise as possible. They had just reached the front of the wagon and were both breathing a sigh of relief when they heard Elizabeth scream.

At once they charged back round the wagon. They found Elizabeth sitting in the back, pointing out across the moonlit landscape.

'There *was* something!' she cried. 'I saw it moving, so clearly this time. I'm sure of it!'

Hattie and John both looked to where she was pointing.

Neither of them could see anything.

'Oh, Lord,' Elizabeth said quietly, putting her hand to her head. 'I just want us all to be safe . . .'

The night remained still, and after a few moments John moved to kiss his wife lightly on the hand. 'We should get back to sleep,' he said. 'Whatever it was must have gone. And we've got another long day tomorrow.'

But, just as John spoke, Hattie gasped and pointed too. 'Wait, Papa! There *is* something out there. Look!'

The moonlight was glinting off an object a short distance away. Whatever it was appeared to be moving closer. As it scuttled into a patch of brighter moonlight, all three Seymours cried out in horror.

What they saw before them was quite unlike anything they had ever seen before. It was a creature like a spider, but it was huge – maybe three feet across. And it was made entirely of metal.

'Back inside the wagon, quick!' John shouted.

But it was too late.

The creature moved so rapidly that there was no time to clamber back into the wagon before it reached them. Hattie could see metal blades protruding from the front of the thing's body. The blades snapped viciously like huge, razor-sharp scissors.

The metal spider braced its legs, then it hurled itself at them.

It struck Hattie full in the chest, knocking her over backwards. She struggled to get up again, but the heavy creature jumped on top of her. The blades protruding from its body snipped together savagely, and its metal legs curled round Hattie so she couldn't move. She would have screamed but, in the face of imminent death, she was too terrified even for that.

Just then, the creature's legs suddenly loosened. Its body

toppled sideways off Hattie's chest and she scrambled back to her feet.

A man she had never seen before was standing close to the spider creature. He was holding what looked like a slim metal tube. The top was lit up, and it was making a bizarre whirring sound. Whatever the tube was, the spider creature certainly didn't like it. Its metal legs thrashed uncontrollably, and smoke began to curl out from the seams in its silver body.

Apparently satisfied with his work, the man slipped the metal tube into his pocket, then turned to the Seymours.

'I'd keep well back if I were you,' he said, his eyebrows scrunching together as he frowned.

Hattie and her father ran to the man, who had taken a few brisk steps backwards.

An instant later, the metal spider exploded in a ball of flame.

They watched it burn for a few moments.

Then John turned to the stranger. 'Who are you?' he asked. 'I mean, we're very grateful for your help and all, but how did you get here? Where on earth did you come from? And what *was* that thing?'

'I'm the Doctor,' the man said. 'Glad to be of service. As for how I got here, well, I imagine the same way you did.'

Hattie looked around. 'I don't see your wagon,' she said,

folding her arms and peering at the man suspiciously.

'Ah,' the Doctor said, running a hand through his grey hair. 'No, I don't have a wagon. Not as such.'

'But you said you got here the same way as us.' Elizabeth, though she seemed shaken, was determinedly climbing down from the wagon to join them.

'I did,' the Doctor admitted. 'The thing is – and I'm sorry if this comes as a bit of a shock – but you didn't come here by wagon either. In fact,' the Doctor went on, raising his eyebrows, 'I very much doubt that *here* is where you think it is.'

'We're on the Oregon Trail,' Hattie told him. 'Where do you think we are?'

The Doctor sighed and sat down on the ground, waving the Seymours to do the same. 'I think you'd all better sit down too. What I'm about to say might come as a bit of a shock.' He appeared to be considering something before adding, 'Well, a *lot* of a shock. Or maybe you just won't understand it at all.'

'I don't understand any of this so far,' Elizabeth said, sitting next to the Doctor. 'You can start by explaining the huge spider thing. What was it?'

'One of the automated crew,' the Doctor replied.

'Crew?' John echoed.

The Doctor gestured for John to be quiet, before going

on. 'You – old-timey, American, human family – were brought here by teleport. The same teleport system interfered with the TARDIS's system and I got diverted here as well.'

'You were right.' Hattie sighed. 'I don't understand a word you just said.'

'Were you travelling alone?' the Doctor went on. 'Just the one wagon?'

'No,' John said. 'There were about a dozen families in our convoy.'

'And what happened to the others?'

'There was a dust storm last night,' Hattie said. 'When we woke up this morning the other wagons had just gone. Disappeared!'

The Doctor nodded, then muttered to himself, 'A dust storm. Yes, that would provide excellent cover for the teleport.'

He sprang back to his feet and pointed at Hattie. 'Tell me,' he said, 'what do you see around you? Apart from your wagon and horses and family and all that stuff.'

'Just the same old dusty landscape. Boring as ever.' Hattie shrugged.

'We came through a valley earlier,' John added. 'Now it's just open grasslands. A few hills in the distance, though you won't see them now because it's too dark. Even with the full moon.'

The Doctor smiled. 'What if I told you that I see something altogether different?'

Hattie's parents looked about as confused as she felt.

'It's difficult to imagine, I know,' the Doctor said. 'I'll see if I can break the conditioning, then perhaps you'll understand.'

'What do you mean "conditioning"?' John asked warily.

'I'm guessing it gets set up during the teleport process,' the Doctor said. He began to pace back and forth in the dust. 'You're conditioned to believe that you're still where you were before the transition. The reality of this place is very different from what you're seeing.'

The Doctor took the metal tube out of his jacket pocket again and started to fiddle with it. 'I think I can overcome the conditioning if I can just find the right frequency . . .'

As the three of them looked on, the Doctor worked at his metal device, frowning intently. It whirred a couple of times and the end lit up again.

Finally, he looked up and smiled. 'That ought to do it.'

'Do *what*?' John asked, throwing his arms up in exasperation.

'Shush. You'll soon see. Now, hold still and look straight ahead.' The Doctor raised the device. 'Oh, and be prepared for a bit of a shock if this works. Which I'm about ninety-nine per cent sure it will.'

The device whirred again and the end glowed blue.

For a moment nothing changed . . . then Hattie felt as if she was falling. Everything went completely and utterly black, just for a few seconds. Then suddenly she could see again.

She was still exactly where she had been – between her parents, looking at the Doctor as he held his strange device, with the wagon behind them – but absolutely everything else had changed.

'But . . .' Elizabeth stood up and spun round in astonishment. 'But this isn't where we were!'

Hattie was too deep in shock to trust herself to speak. She was sitting on a floor made of metal. They were in a vast area that stretched almost as far as she could see. There were metal walls in the distance, and a high vaulted metal roof a long way above their heads.

'Yes,' the Doctor said. 'A bit different from what you were looking at a few moments ago. Sorry about that.' He gestured expansively to the space around them. 'This is where we really are.'

'And where's that?' Hattie managed to whisper.

'To put it in human terms, whoever brought you here has been messing with your heads,' the Doctor said. 'They implanted images of what you expected to see. So, you think you've spent a day driving along the lovely, dusty Oregon

Trail, but you've actually been going round in circles inside
a . . . well, a big metal house, for want of a better term.'

'Why would someone do that?' John asked. 'Are we
in danger? Who trapped my family here, and made us run
round in circles all day?' His hands were curled into fists at
his sides.

'Someone with rather sinister intentions, I'd imagine,'
the Doctor said. 'And, to be precise, it's probably not so much
some*one* as some*thing*.'

The Doctor walked over to the shattered and smoking
remains of the metal spider.

'This creature is not of your Earth,' the Doctor said,
poking it with his shoe. 'And – brace yourselves, because this
is the really juicy part – we're not even on Earth right
now, either.'

There was silence as the Seymours took all this in.

'Not on Earth?' Elizabeth repeated, after what felt like
an age.

'No. We're on a spaceship.' The Doctor saw their
confused looks and sighed. 'A ship that travels among the
stars – or through the heavens, if you like. I'm not sure
exactly where, but somewhere out in the Circes Cluster, I
think. Though that probably doesn't help, does it?'

'Not much,' Hattie huffed, as the Doctor knelt down

beside the remains of the metal spider and peered closely at it.

'Yes,' he said at last. 'I can make a good guess as to why we're here, now. A *very* good guess. This rather unpleasant automaton here looks to me like a product of Belamine technology.'

The Seymours looked at him blankly.

'The Belamines are an alien race,' the Doctor went on. 'That is, they inhabit another planet a long, long way from Earth. Or they did. They inhabit quite a few other planets now. They're colonists.'

Elizabeth laughed, though there was no mirth in it. 'Just like us, then.'

'I suppose, yes,' the Doctor agreed. 'A lot like you, really. We could have a discussion about the rights of Native Americans at this point, but that wouldn't really help matters. The key thing to know is that the Belamines are very aggressive colonists. More like imperialists, really.'

Hattie sighed. 'And in normal English that means?'

'They don't just turn up and found a colony on some other deserted planet. They favour inhabited planets with a local population that can form a slave workforce. Basically, they turn up and invade.'

'And they're going to invade our planet?' John asked, his eyes widening.

The Doctor nodded. 'Yeah, I think that might be the idea,' he said, rather too casually for Hattie's liking.

'So why bring us here?' Elizabeth asked. 'To their . . . ship . . . thing?'

'Well, they're very thorough, the Belamines,' the Doctor told them. 'They like to know all about the planet and the people they're taking on. They're also very pragmatic, which could help us here. If they decide the population might put up too must resistance, they don't bother. They move on to find another, easier world to conquer.' He paused. 'The Belamines always do an assessment,' he said, quieter now. 'And I think they're assessing you.'

Hattie moved closer to her mother and took her hand. She squeezed, and felt Elizabeth squeeze back. Hattie could feel her mother shaking with fear.

'This ship seems to be automated,' the Doctor went on, looking at the mammoth silver space around them. 'I had a good wander around before I found you. There are plenty of those spider things, but no Belamines. I think the ship's task was to bring you here and watch how you behave. The crew – the spider creatures – will produce a report from that, detailing how much of a threat the human race might pose to a Belamine invasion.'

John began to pace back and forth. 'So what can we do?

Are we just stuck here in this metal barn until we starve?'

'No,' the Doctor said. 'I mean, you could just sit here and mope. But I think our best course of action is to convince the Belamines that the human race would fight back, and that they don't want to invade your planet at all.' He smiled. 'So, do you fancy fighting back?'

No one needed long to consider. 'Of course we do.' Elizabeth spoke for them all, her face set with determination.

'Good!' The Doctor grinned, which Hattie thought made him look a little maniacal. 'First we need to get out of this area and see if we can find the main control centre.'

'That doesn't sound too difficult,' John said, as the Seymours rushed after the Doctor, who was striding off across the huge area.

'Yes, I think we'll locate it without too much difficulty,' the Doctor called back over his shoulder. 'It's getting past those robot spiders that will give us the most trouble.'

As they approached the high metal wall, the Doctor continued. 'I saw quite a few on my way in. They didn't seem to notice me, but then I'm not human. They're not monitoring *me*. You, however, are human, so they'll be tracking you wherever you go.'

Hattie looked at her parents. It was a sign of how strange their situation was that neither had so much as blinked when the Doctor referred to himself as 'not human'.

'Why haven't they attacked us already?' John wondered aloud.

'Maybe they think you're just out for a stroll,' the Doctor suggested. 'It's when we break out of this enclosed environment, where they think they've got you trapped, that the fun will really start.'

It didn't sound much like fun to Hattie – but then she remembered how fed up she'd been on the trail, with the same thing happening day in and day out. This was exciting, at least – but also quite terrifying.

Up close, the wall appeared to be one huge, uninterrupted sheet of metal, curving round the entire area without a single break.

'How do we get out?' Elizabeth asked.

'There's a door here somewhere,' the Doctor replied. 'After all, I got in, so there must be a way out.'

He looked first one way along the wall, and then the other.

'Yes,' he decided. 'This way, I think.'

He led them along the wall. Eventually, what looked like a faint join between the metal plates appeared. The Doctor took out the metal tube that he had used to destroy the spider creature.

'Sonic screwdriver,' he explained when he saw the humans scrutinising it. 'If I can just find the right harmonic frequency again . . .'

He adjusted the device and pointed it at the join in the metal. The sonic screwdriver hummed and its tip shone. Then, after a few moments, the join became a gap, as a section of the wall slid away.

'I'll go first, if you don't mind,' the Doctor told them.

The Seymours were more than happy to let the Doctor take the lead. He was, after all, the only one who seemed to know where they were going. He was also the only one with any defence against the spider creatures.

Hattie followed her parents through the gap in the wall. She found herself in a wide corridor also made completely of metal. The Doctor was already making his way cautiously along it, and the Seymours followed close behind him.

'Assuming there's any logic to the layout of this ship,' the Doctor told them, 'the control centre should be this way. It may be quite a distance though,' he warned. 'And those automatons will know you've left the area where you're supposed to be. So get ready to run.'

Hattie assumed that the long word the Doctor had just said meant 'metal spiders'. She looked round warily, but there didn't seem to be any sign of them. Yet.

The corridor came to an end at a metal door. Again the Doctor used his sonic screwdriver to open it – but, as soon as it slid open, Hattie realised they were in deep, deep trouble.

Waiting for them on the other side of the door were three of the spider creatures.

They seemed to have known that the Doctor and the Seymours were coming, because as soon as the door was open wide enough they hurled themselves through it.

One of the spiders hit the Doctor in the chest, knocking him down. His sonic screwdriver flew out of his hand and clattered to the floor. Another of the creatures immediately wrapped itself round John Seymour, squeezing him tight. The third hit Elizabeth on the shoulder and sent her reeling backwards too.

Hattie was momentarily frozen with terror. Then she forced herself to move, and ran to help her father. She tried to pull the spider creature off him, but the thing had its legs wrapped too tightly round him. It was no use.

Hattie looked about, not knowing what to do. The Doctor was sprawled on the ground, grappling with one of the creatures as it slashed its blades at him. Another was scuttling after Hattie's mother as she ran to help the Doctor.

Hattie knew the Doctor, with his sonic screwdriver, was the only one who could stop the spiders. But he had dropped the device – she'd heard it fall to the metal floor. Hattie searched desperately and at last spotted the slim metal tube lying by the wall. She ran and scooped it up.

But what should she do with it now? She had no idea. So she did the only thing she could: she ran over to where the Doctor was still struggling with the creature and, with all the strength she had, shoved it out of the way with her shoulder, pressing the sonic screwdriver into the Doctor's hand.

'Thank you,' the Doctor gasped.

The end of the sonic screwdriver glowed and made its distinctive whirring sound.

At once the spider creature went into spasm. Its legs clenched in tight round its body, and the Doctor hurled it away. A moment later, it exploded into flames, just as the spider that attacked them by the wagon had done.

The Doctor was on his feet immediately. Turning round wildly, he aimed the sonic screwdriver at the creature that was closing in on Elizabeth. He spun away again, pulling Elizabeth with him, before it exploded, then hurried to help John. Together, the Doctor and Hattie managed to detach the spider from him. It dropped to the ground, quick to tense its legs, preparing to leap back at them.

But the Doctor was quicker. As the creature left the ground, it exploded in a ball of fire. John grabbed Hattie and leapt out of the way as the burning creature flew past them and crashed into the wall, to collapse in a flaming heap.

Panting, they all stood and surveyed the burning wreckage of the spiders.

Then the Doctor tucked the sonic away into the pocket of his burgundy jacket.

'Well, that was fun,' he said. 'Let's just hope we don't have too much more of it. I reckon the control centre is just down this corridor. Shall we go and see?'

He didn't wait for a reply, but stomped off through the door and down the corridor beyond. The Seymours followed him. Hattie looked around, alert to any movement, but there was no sign of any more metal spiders. Perhaps, for a minute at least, they'd be safe.

The Doctor stopped a short way ahead of them, and Hattie could see the faint outline of another door.

Grabbing his sonic screwdriver, the Doctor took aim at the door. 'Probably best to keep well back when I open this,' he said jovially. 'Just in case!'

John stood protectively in front of Hattie and Elizabeth as the Doctor opened the door.

Sure enough, behind it was another of the spider creatures.

As it leapt out, Hattie's heart clenched in terror, but the

Doctor was ready for it this time; he caught the thing in mid-air with a pulse from the sonic. The creature was a mass of smoke and flames before it hit the floor.

Immediately the Doctor jumped through the door, holding his sonic screwdriver out in front of him, ready for more spider creatures. After a moment, though, he lowered the sonic and gestured for the others to join him.

Hattie had never seen anything like it before − not even in her most exciting dreams. The room beyond the door was filled with consoles and equipment. Lights flashed and screens displayed images she couldn't understand.

There were several spider creatures in the room, but they all seemed completely preoccupied with the machinery. The Doctor put his finger to his lips.

'I don't think they're designed to fight intruders, unlike their friends,' he whispered. 'They look pretty busy at those controls, so let's leave them to it.'

Hattie and her parents crept as gently as they could behind the Doctor as he made his way round the room, examining everything carefully. Finally, he stopped at a large console and beckoned them over.

'This is the assessment log,' he told them. 'I'll adjust it to erase all mention of myself. That way it'll look like you broke out of the area where they were observing you and destroyed the spider robots all on your own.'

'How will that help?' Elizabeth asked quietly.

'It will make you humans seem clever and dangerous,' the Doctor whispered, with a small smile. 'Too clever and dangerous for the Belamines to risk making an attack and invading Earth.'

'Are you sure it'll work?' John asked seriously, looking hard at the Doctor.

The Doctor nodded, then shrugged. 'Well, I'm sure enough. You lot keep an eye on the spider robots and let me know if any of them start getting agitated. What I need to do takes a bit of skill and a lot of genius. Thankfully, I've got plenty of each.' He wiggled his fingers in the air, then turned to the console and set to work at the main screen.

To Hattie, the time ticked by ever so slowly, as the Doctor hurriedly worked the controls.

There was one worrying moment when a lone spider robot scuttled towards them. Hattie grabbed the Doctor's arm, but he didn't even turn round. He just aimed his sonic screwdriver over one shoulder, straight at the creature, and barely missed a moment of his frantic work as it exploded.

Hattie looked at the smoking ruin lying in the middle of the floor. She was beginning to think this Doctor might be a little bit of a show-off.

After what seemed an eternity, the Doctor turned round and grinned. 'Done,' he said. 'Only one more thing left to do. Or two things, if you count me getting back to my TARDIS.'

'Your what?' Elizabeth asked.

'My TARDIS is how I got here,' the Doctor told them, with a smile. 'And it's how I'll get away again. But, more importantly, the other thing left to do is to get you all home.' He looked around thoughtfully. 'Come over here.'

He led the way across the room to another piece of equipment. In front of it were half a dozen circles marked on the floor.

'Each of you stand in one of those circles,' the Doctor said, already working away at the machine. 'And I'll get you home. Promise.'

Hattie, John and Elizabeth did as they were told and waited.

After some time, the Doctor looked up again.

'I've managed to introduce a slight temporal shift into the transmat beam,' he said, with a small sigh; he looked tired, Hattie thought. 'So you'll arrive back exactly where you were just moments after you left.'

'So we'll still be with the rest of the wagon train?' John asked, exchanging a hopeful glance with Elizabeth.

'Exactly.'

'And what about our wagon and the horses?' Hattie asked.

'Oh, I've sent them back already,' the Doctor said, with an airy wave of his hand. 'Now, this may shake you up a bit, but it's perfectly safe. You'll be home before you know it.'

Hattie opened her mouth to speak – she wanted to say goodbye and thank you to the Doctor, who had saved their lives, after all – but there wasn't time. The breath was suddenly knocked out of her as the Doctor operated the controls in front of him. She felt as if her insides were being pulled out – her vision blurred, and everything went black.

Hattie was lying in her bed in the back of the wagon. She sat up and saw her parents, also sitting up in their beds.

'You know,' Elizabeth said gently, 'I just had the most extraordinary dream.'

'So did I,' John replied, squinting as if trying to recall a lost memory.

Hattie shook her head. 'It wasn't a dream!' She laughed. 'The Doctor was real. I know it!'

Hattie wasn't sure if her family would ever believe that what had happened was real; she wasn't sure that she believed it herself. But she knew she would never complain about being bored again. She had everything she needed, with her family safe and sound and travelling the trail with her.

✦

Millions of miles away and about twenty-four hours later, the Doctor smiled and nodded to himself. A job well done. He turned and walked briskly from the Belamine ship's control centre. In the doorway, he paused and looked back at the spider robots, which were still going about their task, oblivious to his presence.

'Goodbye, chaps,' the Doctor said quietly. 'I can't honestly say it's been a pleasure.'

Then he ran down the corridor, to where he knew the TARDIS was waiting for him.

GHOSTS OF
NEW YORK

It was two months after Mike Tanner died that Pete first saw him again.

It had been a terrible accident: a whole section of the tunnel roof had collapsed suddenly, without any warning. Digging a new subway underneath New York City was always going to be dangerous, but Pete never expected it to be *this* dangerous. He never expected three of his fellow workers to be killed in the process – and he certainly never expected to see one of them again, just a couple of months later.

Pete didn't believe in ghosts. At least, he hadn't believed in ghosts up until that very moment. As he rounded a corner in the tunnel, together with three other subway workers, everything changed: there, standing just ahead of them, was Mike Tanner.

Dead Mike Tanner.

Except, Pete realised with increasing horror, he could see right through Mike; he could make out the details of the tunnel wall behind him. And, perhaps worst of all, Mike was smiling at him. As Pete watched, this ghostly Mike raised a pale, transparent arm and beckoned for Pete to come and join him.

Pete didn't. He did the same as the workers with him: he dropped his tools, turned and ran.

Of course, no one believed their story. By the next day, Pete wasn't even sure if he believed it himself. It must have been his imagination. Surely.

Yet the other three men who had been with him had seen it too: the ghost of poor, dead Mike Tanner standing in the tunnel gesturing to them.

A trick of the light, then? Pete didn't believe that either. But then he didn't really know what he believed any more.

Certainly, no one else thought the story could be true – not until the sightings started happening again and again.

Over the next few days, several more people claimed they had seen Mike Tanner or one of the other victims of the accident. There were reports of other startling, gruesome sightings too. One man said he had seen his long-deceased grandmother standing in a side tunnel. Another was inconsolable after seeing his teenage daughter, who had run away from home, lying on the cold, muddy tunnel floor.

It didn't take long for people to begin to refuse to work in the tunnels. And, once a few refused, more followed their lead. Before long, work on the subway had ground to a halt altogether.

New York in the early 1900s was not one of the Doctor's favourite places, but he supposed he did quite like it. It was a bright morning, so he took a stroll around Central Park – sunglasses on and velvet jacket slung over his shoulder – before heading off to wander the cobbled streets. He paused to look up at some of the taller buildings, shielding his face from the mid-morning sun with his hand. The Empire State Building hadn't been built yet, and he stared up thoughtfully at the space it would one day occupy. He had some interesting memories of a visit to the Empire State Building, but they were memories of events that wouldn't take place for almost thirty years.

On Broadway, the Doctor crossed the road to read the headline on the top newspaper in a stack of them. It was a sensational story: ghosts had supposedly been spotted by workers digging and building the New York Subway.

Intriguing, if a little melodramatic, the Doctor thought.

He bought the paper from the street vendor anyway, and tucked it under his arm to read later – in case he got bored of walking through the city.

It didn't take the Doctor very long to get bored. Or maybe his curiosity about the alleged ghost story just got the better of him. Of course, the Doctor didn't believe everything he read in the papers . . . but he couldn't help wondering if there wasn't some truth in the story. It had made the front page, after all.

He found a park bench at the edge of a small area of green – something of a relief in amongst the grey brick and stone – and sat down to read.

The more the Doctor read, the more curious he became. The report claimed this wasn't just one isolated incident, but the testimony of many workers. If the paper was to be trusted, then it seemed there really were ghosts appearing in New York's brand-new subway tunnels.

The Doctor frowned.

There was definitely something very odd going on.

He scanned the article for any clues as to who was in

charge of the work on the subway, and where they might be located. After a few moments, apparently satisfied that he had the details he needed, he stood up, pulled on his jacket and set off.

It took the Doctor longer than expected to find the office he was looking for. It also took him longer than expected to get an audience with the man in charge of the subway. But, once he did, things went perfectly smoothly – with a little help from his psychic paper.

'Well, what can I say!' the subway boss said, mere minutes after welcoming the Doctor into his office. 'It really is a blessing to have you here, Mr Smith. A renowned psychic investigator, with great successes all across the USA and Europe!'

'And Scotland,' the Doctor reminded him, nodding sagely. 'From seances to exorcisms, I've got all your supernatural requirements covered. You can rest assured.'

Before long, the Doctor had persuaded the subway boss to grant him access to the haunted sections of tunnel so he could investigate the matter of the ghosts. The Doctor promised, in return, that if there were indeed ghosts in the tunnels he would get rid of them. The workers would then be happy to return to digging the subway system.

So, with an official letter of authority, the Doctor set off for the subway tunnels, determined to find out what was really going on under the streets of New York.

If the subway foreman was surprised to see the Doctor, or doubted his alleged credentials, then the letter the Doctor produced immediately put paid to that. Once the foreman had read it, he became animated in his helpfulness, keen to assist in any way he could.

'My good foreman.' The Doctor smiled at the man. 'Would you be so kind as to show me the locations of these sightings?'

Fortunately, after the first few reports of ghosts, the foreman had started keeping a list of sightings and their locations. As the Doctor looked on, the foreman marked the sightings on a map of the subway system – which was simply a map of New York City with the subway tunnels drawn in red over the top.

'Is this all of them?' the Doctor asked.

'There are a couple more that I don't have on my list. I haven't noted the first few that were reported,' the foreman admitted.

Upon the Doctor's instructions, the foreman sent for the first people to see the ghosts.

Four men soon joined them: Pete, who had seen Mike Tanner's ghost; a young man called Tom, who had only been working on the subway for a month; and Dave and Henry, who had also both glimpsed apparitions while working in various tunnels.

The Doctor had each of them add to the map where they had been when they had seen the ghosts. Once they'd finished, the Doctor again inspected the results.

'Interesting,' he said, frowning at the paper. 'The sightings all seem to be clustered in this one area here.' He pointed to an especially busy spot on the map. 'Anything special about the tunnels around there?'

The foreman shrugged. 'Not as far as I know.' He turned to the other men, who were still waiting – and wondering who exactly the Doctor was – but none of them could offer any help.

'It's just part of the tunnel system,' Pete said. 'Nothing special about it. Except for the ghosts, of course.'

'Hmmm,' the Doctor said. 'There's something special about it all right. We just don't know what it is yet.'

'You think you can find out?' the foreman asked.

'I think it's worth a try.' The Doctor jabbed at the map with his finger. 'This section of tunnel is right in the middle of it all, so that's probably the best place to start. Wouldn't you agree, Mr Foreman?'

'I guess so . . .' The foreman didn't sound convinced.

'Good.' The Doctor folded up the map, stuffed it into his coat pocket and grinned at the men. 'If someone can show me the way, I'll get started.'

The foreman eventually persuaded the men to take the Doctor down to the tunnels – but only once he had explained that the Doctor was there to get rid of the ghosts, and even then they were not exactly enthusiastic.

The spot indicated on the map was quite a walk from the entrance. Glowing orange lamps were strung up at intervals along the way, and Pete had brought his own lamp too. Even so, the Doctor had to admit that it was quite spooky down here in the dimly lit, half-built tunnels. If you were going to spot a ghost, then this seemed like the right sort of place for it.

They made their way slowly through the tunnels – only young Tom seemed unsure of the way, which the Doctor put down to his relative inexperience.

Although they chatted and joked, the Doctor could tell that the men were nervous. Perhaps they had cause to be. Whether or not they had really seen ghosts down in the tunnels, it was evident to the Doctor that they had all seen *something* unnerving. And whether that something was truly dangerous or not was yet to be determined . . .

They made a short diversion at one point where the roof had collapsed, blocking the tunnel with rubble and debris. Pete led them down a side tunnel and back to the main route. They splashed through shallow water that was leaking from above, and the Doctor guessed that they were now probably below the water table.

It was a huge undertaking, digging these vast, sprawling tunnels, without any of the useful technology that was to be developed in the years to come. But the Doctor had already travelled on the New York Subway plenty of times, so he knew things would work out in the end.

As they grew ever closer to the section of tunnel the Doctor had wanted to see, the men became quieter and more on edge.

The Doctor paused, wondering if it would help to ask them to recount their experiences. *Probably not*, he thought. But he was curious, so he asked anyway.

Pete told the Doctor about the shimmering apparition of Mike Tanner. The others had similar stories. Tom had seen his father, who had died when Tom was just fourteen. Dave had seen another of the workers killed in the same tunnel collapse as Mike. Henry said he had seen his great-uncle, who used to live with his family.

'There's no question about it,' he said, firm and resolute. 'It was him. I knew the old man well.'

If anything, the men seemed a little more relaxed after relating their experiences. The Doctor thanked them, and they pressed on, to the very epicentre of whatever this phenomenon really was.

'We're almost there,' Pete announced at last, a slight tremor in his voice. 'The spot you wanted to see is just past the next intersection, Doctor. One left turn and you're there.'

The Doctor peered ahead into the dark tunnel. 'You've been very helpful,' he said. 'All of you.'

'You reckon you can get rid of these ghosts, Doctor?' Dave asked. 'Or whatever they are.'

'They're ghosts,' Henry said. 'That's all there is to it.'

The Doctor smiled, not wanting to discourage any of the men. 'Experience has taught me that there are many different kinds of so-called ghosts. Once I know which variety these are, I can work out what to do about them.'

'Rather you than me,' Tom said quietly.

As they reached the intersection and the final left turn, Pete stopped dead with a gasp.

The others collided into one another behind him.

The Doctor's eyes widened. 'Well, this mystery just got very interesting indeed.'

In the tunnel ahead of them stood a figure. It was sort of there and yet not there at the same time. It looked substantial – but, at the same time, the Doctor could see right through it.

'It's Mike Tanner,' Pete said, his breath coming in panicked gasps. 'Just like before. He was killed, I promise you. I saw it happen months ago!'

The Doctor frowned, clearly deep in thought. 'How fascinating,' he murmured.

He bent down and picked up a rock from the tunnel floor.

'What are you doing?' Dave hissed.

'Just a quick experiment,' the Doctor said. Then he flung the rock at the figure in front of them.

The rock passed right through Mike Tanner and hit the wall behind. It rattled down the curved rock and hit the tunnel floor.

'I'm not going another step,' Henry said, his voice quavering. 'You wanted to get to this place, and here you are. You're on your own now, Doctor!'

'I agree,' Dave said. 'I'm getting out of here! Pete?'

'I can't stay here, Doctor,' Pete croaked, shaking his head.

All three of them backed away.

The Doctor turned to them in surprise and exasperation. 'But I've just proved that there's nothing of substance to him!' he said. Then he added, more gently,

'Truthfully, I could use your help.'

'I'm sorry,' Pete said. 'Really, I am.'

Then he, Dave and Henry turned and ran back the way they had come.

Tom, however, hadn't moved. He was still staring wide-eyed at the ethereal figure in the tunnel.

'You're not going with your friends, then?'
the Doctor asked.

Tom shook his head. 'Oh, I'm frightened enough,' he admitted. 'Terrified, even. But I want to know what's going on, Doctor – and I think my best chance of finding out is to stick with you.'

'Good lad.' The Doctor patted him on the shoulder. 'I know you're afraid, but this chap here seems docile enough. So I think we're safe. For now.'

Tom nodded, pale and frightened. 'So, what do we do? Talk to him?'

'I doubt he can answer,' the Doctor said. 'He probably can't hear us. He may not even know who he is.'

'Then what's he doing here?'

'Who knows? Something is causing these apparitions. Once we know what that something is, we can make sure the ghosts disappear – and never come back!'

The Doctor squinted at the wall of the tunnel and began

poking it in various places. He turned and looked at Tom
with narrowed eyes, as if appraising him. 'You up to having a
hunt around? To see what we can discover?'

'All right.' Tom took a few deep breaths, gathering his
courage, then followed the Doctor slowly down the tunnel,
towards the ghost of Mike Tanner.

As they stepped forward cautiously in the gloom, the
Doctor rummaged in his pockets. He made a noise of triumph
and brought out a small metal box with a dial on the top.

Tom wanted to ask what it was, but they had almost
reached the ghostly form of Mike Tanner. So, instead, he
kept his eyes firmly on the figure, ready to make a run for it if
it so much as twitched.

Mike's ghost remained perfectly still as they walked
right past.

Tom breathed a small sigh of relief, then looked at the
Doctor. He seemed entirely uninterested in the ghost itself,
and was instead preoccupied with his metal device.

'It's just a meter,' the Doctor said, noticing Tom
watching. 'It detects emissions, power sources, that sort of
thing.' He paused and tapped the box, frowning at the dial on
the top, gave it a shake, then nodded. 'This way.'

The Doctor strode on until they came to another side
tunnel, then he consulted the box again. After a brief bit of

spinning on the spot, he pointed on and continued straight forwards.

After a few paces, though, Tom stopped abruptly. His heart began to hammer against his ribcage.

'Doctor . . .' he said quietly.

The Doctor had been staring down at his box. He looked up at Tom, his brow furrowed. 'What now?'

Tom pointed down the tunnel ahead of them.

'More ghosts,' he said, his voice a whisper and his breath clouding in the cold air.

Further down the tunnel, as if waiting for them, stood more pale figures – several elderly men and women, and a girl no older than fourteen or fifteen. They illuminated the dark space around them with a light, silvery glow, their faces expressionless.

The Doctor smiled, his grin made eerie by the glow of the spirits. 'Excellent. This means we're getting close. On the other hand –' He paused.

'On the other hand what?' Tom whispered.

'Whatever we're looking for seems to be guarded. The thing making these ghosts doesn't want us to find it.' He shrugged. 'Well, at least we'll soon have our answers, won't we? Come along, Tom!'

He grabbed the young lad by the arm and pulled him

towards the transparent figures. As they began to weave a
path between the ghosts, Tom whispered urgently to the
Doctor, 'What are they made of, Doctor? Can you tell yet?'

This time, the figures turned to watch as they passed, but
they didn't move to stop them.

The Doctor paused, peering closely at one ghost's silvery
sleeve, then, in a sudden surge of bravery, touched it with one
outstretched finger.

The ghost seemed to melt, just for a second, in the spot
he had touched it.

He narrowed his eyes, apparently making a mental note,
then moved on.

'They're not ghosts,' the Doctor told Tom. 'Not in the
wandering-spirits-of-dead-people sense. They're more
like projections.'

'Projections?'

'Yes, you know, like a movie.' Tom looked at him blankly.
The Doctor sighed. 'Too early for you, I suppose . . .
A Kinetoscope, then. Ever seen one of those?'

Tom nodded. 'A long time ago. Who's projecting them?'

'Not sure.' The Doctor stepped sideways round the
ghost of a man in his sixties. 'I'd say the tunnelling here has
disturbed something buried deep in the ground beneath New
York City. Something that doesn't want to be found by you

industrious humans. You're always digging up ancient stuff so
you can zip faster from one place to another.'

He checked his metal box again as they stepped into
a small area by the wall and away from the ghosts. 'So, the
energy source would seem to be about . . . here.'

He pointed to a spot on the wall.

Tom could see nothing remarkable about it, but the
Doctor was already tearing wooden planks away to reveal
earth banked up behind.

'We need a spade or a pickaxe or something,' the Doctor
said, standing back to admire the damage he'd already done.

Tom looked around. 'I did see a spade earlier,' he
recalled. 'I guess someone panicked when they saw the ghosts
and dropped it.'

'Off you pop to get it, then!' the Doctor said cheerily,
rummaging in his pockets once more.

Tom set off back down the tunnel. Sure enough, the
spade was exactly where he remembered. He grabbed it and
hurried back to the Doctor, trying to ignore the watching
ghosts as he slipped past them.

'Here.' Tom held out the spade, but the Doctor shook
his head.

'I imagine you'll be better at digging than I am.' He
pointed to the hole in the wall. 'Just go for it, in that general

area, and we'll see what we find.'

Tom was beginning to feel a little exasperated with the
Doctor, but he set to work anyway, pushing the spade deep
into the side of the tunnel. To his surprise, it passed easily
through the earth for a few inches – then it stopped dead.

'Problem?' the Doctor asked.

'I think I've hit a stone or something,' Tom said, pulling
the spade out.

'Or something,' the Doctor said quietly. 'All right. Let's
see what's in there.'

Tom dug away at the wall. Whatever his spade had hit
was larger than any stone he'd come across before. It seemed
to occupy the whole area he was digging. The earth piled up at
their feet, and Tom stared in surprise at what he had uncovered.

The Doctor, however, simply nodded and smiled as if
this was exactly what he had been expecting. He reached
out and rapped his knuckles on the solid object. It was a
translucent blue material, a shiny sapphire surface that
was hard to the touch yet looked organic somehow – like a
mineral that had grown there in the earth.

Tom reached out cautiously to touch the bright blue
surface. As he did so, the whole section he had cleared shifted,
sliding open, mud falling to the floor as it moved. He pulled
his hand away quickly.

'Oh, well done, Tom!' the Doctor cried.

'What did I do?' Tom gasped.

'You must have touched a control point,' the Doctor replied. 'It's a hatchway!'

'Like on a ship?' Tom said, confused.

'Exactly like on a ship!' the Doctor said, sounding utterly delighted with their discovery.

Tom looked into the darkness beyond the hatch. As he watched, soft blue lights inside began to glow, flickering into life.

'Hmm. Someone knows we're here,' the Doctor said. 'Looks like they're on emergency power only, though. I'd guess this ship has been here for quite a while.'

He jumped gleefully through the hatchway, then stuck his head back out into the tunnel.

'Are you coming or not?' he asked Tom.

Tom gulped. It would be a step into completely unknown territory – but so far the Doctor had been right about everything, and he didn't seem afraid. Tom had already walked through a crowd of ghosts today. He doubted things could get much more bizarre.

He took a deep breath and stepped through the hatchway after the Doctor.

Tom found himself standing in a corridor rather like one of the smaller tunnels in the subway system, except it was made entirely from the same blue material as the hatch. In places the walls and floor were solid and crystal-like, shiny and glimmering; in others, soft and fleshy, like a gigantic sea urchin.

The Doctor didn't appear to think this was unusual at all.

He beckoned to Tom and led the way down the corridor, and Tom nervously followed.

After a while, they reached a door. The Doctor pressed his hand against a panel of squashy matter, which glowed with a deep midnight-blue light, positioned to one side of the door.

The door slid open to let them through.

'Is this all there is? Corridor after corridor?' Tom asked as they started along another brilliant turquoise corridor.

'I doubt it,' the Doctor told him. 'This ship has just been here an awfully long time. I imagine it crash-landed, or stopped here by accident. Now it's dormant – waiting for someone to tell it what to do.'

They crept forward, the air around them electric with tension, every one of Tom's senses on high alert.

'Doctor,' he whispered. 'If this is a ship . . . what happened to the crew?'

'Maybe it's an automated craft. Maybe they were killed in the crash.' The Doctor grinned. 'Or maybe we'll meet them soon.'

As they walked on, the Doctor continued to muse

aloud. 'The ghosts – they're a defence mechanism. The ship doesn't want to be found or interfered with, so it looks into the memories of anyone who comes close. It then draws on a particularly powerful memory – and memories of death or the loss of someone you knew or loved are always powerful – and projects that memory. As a ghost.'

They had reached yet another door.

'Now, *this* is more like it,' the Doctor announced, as he pushed it open.

They stepped into a long chamber, so long that Tom could only just see the wall at the furthest end, the roof arching high above his head. All along the walls were what looked like cubicles, each curtained off with some sort of semi-transparent membrane. He could just make out dark shapes beyond. Everything looked like it was fashioned from the same blue organic material as the hatch and the corridors. It was, Tom noticed, even colder here than the rest of the ship.

'What is this place?' Tom whispered.

The Doctor was surveying what they'd found with narrowed eyes. 'A tourist ship,' he said. 'I should've guessed. And these must be the tourists themselves.' He gestured to the cubicles.

'You mean there are people in there?'

'Well,' the Doctor said. 'They might be people. More

likely they're a completely different species.'

He sighed, and Tom thought he saw a sudden darkness appear in the Doctor's expression.

'They were probably off to visit some fantastic planets, incredible stars, galaxies light-years away . . . A trip to see the sights of the universe. What a waste of life.'

The Doctor began to walk across the chamber.

'They were cryogenically frozen for the journey,' the Doctor murmured. 'For centuries or longer. Except, of course, they never arrived at their destination.'

He turned to Tom and, seemingly for his benefit, began to elaborate.

'They're asleep. The journey is so long that the passengers are put to sleep for the duration, frozen in time. Then, when the ship arrives at its destination, they're woken up again. Saves food, supplies and an awful lot of boredom.' He walked over to one of the cubicles. 'Only these poor passengers are never going to wake up.'

The Doctor reached out and grabbed the edge of the membrane covering the cubicle in front of him. Then, in a single sharp movement, he pulled it away. He stood aside so that Tom could see past him and into the cubicle.

Inside was a husk. A dried, desiccated figure, curled up as if asleep. But it was quite obviously not sleeping; it was dead and, from the near-mummified condition of the body, had been for a very long time.

Tom was horrified, though he tried not to show it.

'Automated systems – they've been left running, despite the fact that no one on board is alive,' the Doctor continued. 'We need to find some central controls to shut this ship down for good. If we turn off the defence mechanism, the ghosts should vanish.'

The Doctor looked sadly around the entire chamber.

'How we deal with this lot, I'm not sure. The technology is far too advanced for this time period, as I'm sure you've noticed. We can't let anyone else find it. One human witness is quite enough.'

'Could we just bury it again?' Tom asked, trying not to think too hard about what the Doctor had just said. Did he really have to be the only human who knew the truth? That life existed on incredible planets far away from Earth, and that it had travelled here?

The Doctor grimaced. 'We could, but sooner or later I suspect someone else would dig it up. No, I need to think of a more permanent solution . . . preferably one that doesn't destroy New York City.' He frowned. 'First, though, let's shut down our ghostly friends. That way!'

The Doctor pointed across the vast chamber to where

Tom could just make out another door, then started running towards it. Tom hurried to catch up.

'You know a lot about this place,' he said, jogging alongside the Doctor.

'I suppose I do.'

'You're not really just an exorcist or psychic researcher or whatever you said you were, are you?'

'No,' the Doctor admitted. 'I'm a lot more than that. But don't worry about it. We'll get this sorted out, and then you can go back to digging your subway with no further problems. Well, not from ghosts, anyway.'

'I'm not sure I want to be digging tunnels again after all this,' Tom said, as they reached the door.

The Doctor put his hand on the squashy panel to the side and the door slid open. 'Nonsense,' he said. 'The New York Subway will be magnificent when it's finished. You should be proud to be involved.'

Tom had no idea how the Doctor could know that for certain, but there was no time to ask; the Doctor was already stepping through the doorway.

'Ah, here we are,' he said. 'The nerve centre of the ship!'

Tom wasn't sure what to expect from a nerve centre, but this room had walls covered in panels of controls and a huge column covered in lights at its centre. The entire room was pulsing with energy, soft blue patches of organic cabling intertwined with gemstone operating panels, all glowing with a distinctly non-human life force. There were translucent screens on which lines and lines of mysterious symbols were displayed, none of which meant anything to Tom.

The Doctor seemed to understand it all, however.

He walked slowly round the room, examining everything, and occasionally nodding and smiling. Finally, he stopped and pointed to a collection of controls.

'I think this is what we need. I just have to check something first.'

He took the map of the subway tunnels out of his pocket and flattened it out across the top of a metal table.

'This is where we were when we entered through the hatch, yes?' the Doctor said, pointing to a spot on the tunnel system marked over the map of New York.

Tom looked where the Doctor was pointing. 'Yes,' he agreed. 'That's it.'

'So above us now is what?' The Doctor squinted at the map.

'Nothing,' Tom told him. 'That whole area's been cleared for a new building, but they haven't started work on it yet. It's just a wasteland. Empty ground.'

The Doctor smiled and closed his eyes, sighing gently.

'Well, Tom. Isn't that marvellous? Sometimes miracles really do happen.'

He scrunched the map up and stuffed it back into his pocket.

'Why is that good?' Tom asked. 'The ship is buried way down here! Who cares what's on the surface?'

'You'll see,' the Doctor said cryptically, and he set to work at the controls.

As he worked, Tom looked back at the door nervously. With a chill, he realised that they were no longer alone.

Dozens of faint figures had formed out of the air, and all were moving to stand beside the Doctor. Ghosts. More of them than ever.

'Doctor,' Tom said. 'We've got company.'

The Doctor looked up. He saw the ghosts and smiled.

'Oh, don't worry,' he said. 'They're just trying to scare us off. They think I'm trying to sabotage the ship. Though actually it's quite the opposite – I'm trying to get it working again!'

The Doctor carried on fiddling and jabbing at seemingly random panels, ignoring the increasing number of ethereal figures gathering around him.

Tom nervously backed towards a wall. 'They can't hurt us, can they?'

'No, they're harmless. I'm sure of it,' the Doctor said, without looking up. 'I doubt they can even touch us.'

As the Doctor spoke, one of the ghostly figures reached out and grabbed his arm, pulling it away from the controls.

'Then again, I could be wrong about that,' the Doctor said. He pulled himself free and staggered away, before throwing himself back towards the controls.

'What do we do?' Tom yelled, as another wave of ghosts moved even closer.

'You keep them busy while I finish what I'm doing,' the Doctor said, sounding a little panicked. 'Can you manage that?'

Tom gulped and nodded. 'I can try.'

'Good lad!'

The ghosts were now tightly clustered around the Doctor. Tom grabbed at the nearest of them, expecting his hand to go right through it, but, to his surprise, the ghost felt solid – as if it had toughened up in preparation for a fight. Tom caught hold of the ghost's arm and pushed it away. It knocked over a few other ghosts behind it.

Meanwhile, Tom had grabbed at another, pulling it as hard as he could away from the Doctor. Then he leapt back and pushed a third ghost hard in the chest, hoping for a repeated domino effect.

It seemed like more ghosts were fading into existence

every second. Tom did his best to keep them away from the Doctor; he pushed and shoved, doing anything he could to give the Doctor time and space.

At last, the Doctor looked up. 'Right,' he said. 'That's it!'

He turned and pushed past several of the ghosts, then headed towards the door.

'We have to get out of here. Fast!' he yelled.

'Why the rush?' Tom gasped, as they ran back through the chamber full of cubicles and into the corridor beyond. Behind them, the ghosts followed, but it seemed they could only glide at a slow pace. They started to fizzle out, one by one, and Tom wondered if they'd soon be reappearing ahead to block their path.

'I worked out from the navigation systems where this ship came from,' the Doctor told him as they ran. 'So I'm sending it back home. I got the main systems back online and set the course.'

They reached the outer hatchway and leapt through it. As soon as they were back in the subway tunnel, the Doctor produced a metal tube from his pocket and pointed it at the hatchway. It emitted a buzzing noise and a blue glow, and the hatchway was closed again. Then he grabbed Tom's arm and together they sprinted down the tunnel, away from the ship.

'As there's only waste ground above,' the Doctor explained breathlessly, 'the ship won't do any damage when it leaves.'

'What? You mean it's going to burst up through the ground?' Tom's words were drowned out by an explosion of sound from behind them.

The Doctor shouted over the noise, which was growing louder. 'Main engines still work. It'll blast its way out of the ground, and up through the atmosphere of your tiny little planet. Then it'll follow the course I set. Goodness knows what the people back home will make of it turning up again after all this time. If there's anyone still there, that is.'

Tom glanced back over his shoulder towards the noise, which was by now louder than anything he had ever heard in his life. In the distance, at the end of the tunnel, he could see a ball of flame. It seemed to be getting bigger, and it was definitely heading towards them.

He picked up the pace, running as fast as he could, feeling the heat of the flames on his back, and amazed at the blistering pace the Doctor was managing to set.

They reached the entrance to the main tunnel system, and ran up the wooden steps that led to ground level. They emerged, blinking, into the sunlight.

The Doctor stopped, breathing heavily. He slapped Tom on the back.

'Thanks for all your help,' he said.

'Pleasure,' Tom told him, also catching his breath. 'Though I still don't really know what we did.'

In answer, the Doctor pointed across the city. 'Look over there. You've got a front-row seat.'

Tom looked to where the Doctor was pointing.

After a few moments, a towering streak of fire erupted from the ground and blasted its way up into the sky. It kept going until it was out of sight, and a shower of mud and stone fell in great clouds on to the buildings around it.

'The ship flies again!' the Doctor cried. 'On its way back home at last. We did a good thing there, Tom.' He paused and sighed. 'But the important thing is that we got rid of the ghosts. That's probably all you need to tell anyone else. Understand?'

As Tom nodded, several other figures came running up to him and the Doctor. It was Pete, Dave and Henry; it now felt like a lifetime ago that they had left the Doctor and Tom down in the tunnels.

'Tom! And, Doctor! I'm sorry we left you. It was a cowardly thing to do,' Pete said, his face ashen. 'We were about to come back and find you when that thing blasted out of the ground!'

'Don't worry,' the Doctor said. 'We got rid of your

ghosts for you. They're gone for good.'

He reached out and shook hands first with Pete, and then with Dave and Henry too. Finally, he shook Tom's hands.

'You take care of yourself,' the Doctor said. 'All of you. Especially you, Tom. You've been particularly brave.'

Then, with that, he turned on his heel and started to walk away.

'Doctor!' Tom called. 'You're not coming to tell the foreman that the ghosts have gone?'

Whether the Doctor heard him or not, Tom wasn't sure. Either way, the Doctor didn't turn back.

'Tom,' Pete asked. 'What exactly happened down there?'

'And what the heck was that explosion?' Dave chipped in. 'And that fire in the sky?'

But Tom was too distracted to answer; as he watched the Doctor walk away, he wondered who on earth the strange man really was, and whether he'd ever be lucky enough to meet him again.

TAKING THE PLUNGE

The Doctor quite liked theme parks. He wasn't all that sold on the various rides, but it pleased him to see people enjoying themselves.

It was hot and humid under the Florida sun, and the Doctor was starting to feel the effects. He found himself a bench in the shade, and settled in to watch the tourists at Adventure World milling excitedly around.

Though it soon became obvious that not everyone was enjoying themselves. The Doctor looked on with amusement as a teenager whined to her parents about how boring it was here, while her younger sister, who was occasionally letting out high-pitched squeaks behind her, seemed barely able to contain her excitement.

Well, the Doctor thought, *there's always someone who doesn't want to have a good time.*

At the opposite extreme, a young boy of about ten, whom the Doctor had just spotted, was so thrilled to be there that he kept bouncing up and down, then running off to look at different things. His parents, trailing after him, were noticeably frustrated. The Doctor watched as the three of them made their way round the area where he was sitting, then disappeared in the direction of another ride.

After a while, the Doctor got up from his shady seat and set off on a stroll through the park. He paused to look in a gift shop, and stopped to get himself an ice cream.

The Doctor loitered to watch the various rides – the ones he could see, that is. Some were indoors, so the only way to experience them was to actually go on them. 'I'm at least five centuries too old for that,' the Doctor muttered to himself. Besides, he knew a ride in the TARDIS was far more exciting – and unpredictable – than any of the rides on offer here.

Though he probably wouldn't have admitted it, the Doctor was having a pleasant day. It was good to have a bit of a break. Here in this world of rides and gift shops and ice creams everyone – even the Doctor – was far away from the cares and woes of everyday life.

Just then, the Doctor spied something that made him

wonder if everything was quite as perfect as it seemed. Among the hordes of theme-park goers, he spotted the family with the hyperactive ten-year-old boy again. They were walking back through the park, towards the Doctor – only dramatically changed from when he had last seen them.

The boy's mother and father looked completely worn out. As they shuffled past the Doctor, he noticed dark shadows beneath their eyes, which were glazed over with tiredness. Possibly to be expected, given how the boy had been rushing about earlier, the Doctor supposed.

But then the boy too seemed quiet and lethargic. He wasn't bouncing around or rushing off any more. Instead, he was ambling silently and slowly along beside his parents, a similarly glassy look in his eyes.

Such a pronounced change in such a short space of time is distinctly odd, the Doctor thought. Yes, there was something wrong here, he was sure of it. And he was going to find out exactly what it was.

'Hello,' he said cheerily, catching up with the family.

'Oh. Hello,' the father said glumly, stopping and turning slowly to face the Doctor. 'Do we know you?'

'No, I don't think so,' the Doctor said. 'But I saw you earlier. Your son seemed to be enjoying himself.'

'He was,' the mother replied. She and the little boy had

also stopped. 'Weren't you, Dan?'

The boy mumbled a reply, which the Doctor didn't quite catch.

'Seems to have lost some of his enthusiasm since then,' the Doctor observed.

'I think we all have,' the father said. 'Probably reached our limit. We've been here since the place opened this morning.'

'I hadn't realised it would be so tiring,' the mother complained. 'I'm exhausted, and all we've done is sit on rides and walk around the park.'

'Is that right?' the Doctor said, raising one quizzical eyebrow. 'Did you get tired suddenly?'

'Well, yes, actually,' the mother said. 'We did.' She looked a little confused.

'All of you?' the Doctor asked. He was thoroughly intrigued now. 'At the same time?'

'I guess so,' the father said. 'I mean, I noticed Dan here calming down. He got very quiet. Then it hit me how tired I was feeling – how tired we all were. We must have been overdoing things.'

'We're going to go and have a rest and a snack,' the mother said. 'We'll all feel better after that, won't we?'

'Possibly,' the Doctor said, but he didn't look convinced.

'Can you just tell me,' he added, stopping them as they made to leave, 'when was it exactly that you began to feel so tired?'

'Um, I think it was after that last ride,' the mother said.

'Or maybe during it,' the father added. 'But yes, sometime around then – that's when it hit me. Dan didn't seem so excited afterwards, even though it's a great ride. One of the best.'

'Maybe I should give it a go,' the Doctor said. 'Which ride was it?'

'I can't remember what it was called,' the mother said. 'Space something, I think – wasn't it, Dan?'

The boy looked up. He had dark rings under his eyes; he really did look incredibly tired. The Doctor crouched down so he was at eye level with the child.

'Do you remember the name of the ride?' the Doctor asked gently.

Dan nodded. 'Space Plunge,' he said, pointing back the way they had come. 'It's over there. They whizz you round and round in the dark in a little cart past stars and planets and stuff. Then you drop really fast. It makes your stomach go all wobbly.'

'I bet it does,' the Doctor said, straightening up once more. 'Thank you,' he said to the family, then added, 'I hope you feel better once you've eaten something.'

'So do I,' the mother said, but the Doctor was already darting off in the direction the boy had pointed.

It wasn't difficult to find Space Plunge. It was in a huge, tall building with a rocket rising from the roof. The rocket was the sort you would see in a 1950s B-movie – which is to say, to the Doctor's expert eyes, completely impractical. Nevertheless, the exterior of the Space Plunge building suggested adventure; what, after all, could be more adventurous than space travel?

A long queue snaked out of the entrance to the building, and the Doctor joined the back of it.

The line moved slowly, giving the Doctor time to wonder if this was really worth it. All he had seen was one family worn out after a long morning at a theme park. Was there really anything unusual about that? But the little boy had been so full of energy earlier on. Definitely something strange in that, the Doctor decided. And he was almost certain that this Space Plunge had something to do with it.

Finally, the Doctor found himself at the front of the queue. He was ushered to a small cart on a track, with room for six people. The Doctor took his place in the front beside a mother and her delighted daughter. Behind them were three noisy teenage boys, who also seemed thrilled at the prospect of the ride. They pushed each other boisterously, good-naturedly teasing each other about who was the most afraid.

It started fairly sedately. The cart rolled along the track into utter blackness. Gradually, stars – or, rather, lights that were meant to look like stars – appeared above them. The cart picked up speed, rolling up and down inclines, and taking sudden turns as it whizzed past illuminated model planets.

The passengers in the cart with the Doctor seemed to be enjoying themselves. They cried out and even screamed as the cart dipped and rolled suddenly. As for the Doctor, he found the ride interesting, but not terribly exhilarating. He wondered how long the whole thing would last.

At last it seemed that the ride was reaching its grand finale. The cart tipped backwards and headed uphill.

I think I can guess what's coming next, the Doctor thought. There was a reason why it was called Space Plunge, after all.

Sure enough, at that moment, the cart levelled out. It stopped for an instant, poised in space, then slowly tipped forward . . . and dropped like a stone. The others in the cart screamed with terror and excitement. *Humans*, the Doctor thought, as his stomach lurched uncomfortably. *So easily entertained.*

Eventually, the cart reached the bottom of its plunge

and the track flattened out again. The cart trundled forward benignly at half the speed it had been going. As they rolled past a model planet, and were bathed in its glow, the Doctor saw that everyone else in the cart suddenly looked drawn and tired. They were completely silent; no more shouting and screaming, despite the adrenaline rush they'd just experienced. They seemed every bit as exhausted as the family the Doctor had seen out in the park.

As for the Doctor, he felt no different at all. *Now that*, he thought, *is interesting*.

As soon as he had exited the Space Plunge building, the Doctor found a point from which he could watch both the queue for the ride and the people leaving it. Comparing the two, he noticed a distinct difference. The people waiting for the ride appeared eager, ready to give it a try, while everyone leaving it looked subdued. And not just some people, but *everyone*.

This, to the Doctor's mind, could not be a coincidence. The ride was not terrifying or demanding enough to have that effect on people. 'No,' the Doctor mumbled to himself. 'There's something else going on here. Time to work out what it is.'

He thought back over the ride. It seemed as if the people

in the cart with him had suddenly lost their energy in the final plunge.

'I need to get into the building to examine the ride!' he said loudly. A few people standing near to him looked his way, startled. He waved them off with a dismissive bat of his hand. If he could find the point where Space Plunge actually plunged, he reasoned, then he was sure he could work out what was going on.

The Doctor raced back over to the building and skidded to a halt. He walked around the ride's outer wall slowly, trying to appear casual. 'There must be a maintenance entrance here somewhere,' he muttered. Space Plunge would need to be checked and serviced, and maintenance workers would have to be able to get inside to fix it if anything went wrong.

'Aha!' The Doctor had found a small door set in the side of the building, well away from the entrance and exit to the ride. The door was locked, of course – but it didn't take him long to open it with his sonic screwdriver.

He looked around to make sure no one was watching, then he pulled open the door and slipped through, quietly closing it behind him.

Inside, it was almost completely dark. The only illumination came from the faint glow of the points of light that were meant to be stars and from the model planets.

Holding his sonic screwdriver in front of him as a torch, the Doctor tried to work out where exactly he was in relation to the ride high above him.

As it turned out, it was fairly easy to find the track – the Doctor was able to make out the dark silhouettes of carts rushing along it. He heard the train going clattering by too, accompanied by the shouts and screams of its passengers.

Now that he knew where the track was, all he had to do was follow it to the point where it plunged. Keeping the sonic screwdriver glowing so that he could see where he was putting his feet, he climbed his way carefully across the building.

Following the excited shrieks of the carts' passengers, the Doctor made his way to the point where the track suddenly dipped. The volume of the passengers' cries rose considerably as he approached, and at last he could see the silhouettes of the carts falling steeply from a huge height, before the track levelled out and disappeared through the exit. Just as they slowed down again, the carts fell noticeably silent. Whatever was going on, it was happening right here at the plunge.

The Doctor scanned the area with his sonic, hunting for anything giving off a suspicious emission, or anything that wasn't native to Earth in this time period. It didn't take the sonic screwdriver long to detect something – and that something was attached to the underside of the track.

There was just one problem: it was situated a fair way up the steep final drop.

The Doctor looked around for a way to reach it. He didn't fancy trying to climb the track. Not only was it a long way up, but if he climbed up the back of the track, the carts dropping down could slice off his fingers. Not an appealing option.

Fortunately, there was another solution. Shining his sonic ahead of him in the darkness, the Doctor made out the vague shape of a scaffolding tower. The track was fixed to the scaffolding at various points to give it stability and, as he looked more closely, the Doctor noticed the tower had ladders and narrow walkways.

He pushed his sonic screwdriver back into his pocket. His eyes had at last adjusted to the darkness enough that he could see what he was doing without it.

Hunting around at the base of the tower, the Doctor eventually found a ladder. He climbed until he reached a narrow platform where he could stand and watch the track dropping in front of him, into the darkness. Just then, a cart hurtled past, so close he could feel the breeze on his face as the excited shrieks of the passengers rang in his ears.

Taking extreme care not to get in the way of any more carts, he examined the underside of the track – but there was nothing attached to it.

So, the Doctor climbed up to the next platform, and
again inspected the track. Still no sign of anything unusual –
certainly nothing to explain the readings his sonic had picked
up. The Doctor set off to the next walkway, wondering how
many ladders he would have to climb before he finally found
whatever it was he was looking for.

At the next level, he had more luck. It was well
disguised, and a cursory glance might well have missed it,
but the Doctor's keen eyes detected something attached to
the underside of the track – something that most definitely
should not have been there.

He peered closely at it through the gloom.

What he saw was a series of metal boxes, linked together
by wires. He took his sonic screwdriver out of his pocket and
set to work trying to discover what the boxes actually did.

The first one turned out to be a power relay. Boring, but
perhaps he could trace where the power was going to, and so
work out which of these boxes was the most important . . .

The next box was far more interesting. The circuitry and
components inside it were unlike anything the Doctor had
seen before – at least not assembled in this way. He recognised
most of the elements, though, and he had seen firsthand how
the carts' passengers were affected as they plunged. It didn't
take a genius to work out what the box was actually doing.

It was draining the very life essence of the passengers as they passed over it.

That was why they suddenly became tired.

The box used a form of mental induction, and, since the Doctor himself had not been affected by it, was obviously locked on to human biological make-up. As for the other boxes, it seemed they were channelling the energy drained from the carts' passengers.

But where is the energy being sent? the Doctor thought, growing more frustrated by the second. He couldn't see anything to indicate where it was going – but it was definitely being routed away from here, and presumably stored somewhere too.

The Doctor wasn't sure of the purpose behind this exercise, but draining humans of their life essence was wrong. Whoever was doing it had to be stopped. *They won't get away with it,* the Doctor thought. *Not on my watch.*

He set to work fiddling with the box. Once he had figured out what all the various components did, the Doctor began the task of getting them to do something different.

One of the components seemed to store the DNA signature of everyone who passed by and had their energy drained. It wasn't clear to the Doctor *why* exactly it would do that. What it *did* mean, though, was that, with a bit of luck and a lot of cleverness, he could reverse the flow and channel the energy back to them. Whatever could be made to flow in one direction could almost always be persuaded to flow back in the other again.

It was meticulous work, but eventually the Doctor reckoned he was done. He sealed up the boxes again, admiring his own handiwork.

Now all he had to do was find whoever was responsible for this devious scheme. But as it happened, he Doctor didn't need to worry about finding the culprit at all.

While he stood there, pondering his next course of action, the culprit found him.

Hearing footsteps approaching along the platform, the Doctor turned and found himself face-to-face with a rather ordinary-looking middle-aged man in overalls. What was rather less ordinary about the man was that he was holding a gun, and pointing it at the Doctor.

'Who are you?' the man demanded.

'I'm the Doctor,' the Doctor told him. 'And *who* are *you?*'

'My name's Tunbridge,' the man replied. 'I work in maintenance.'

'Do you now?' The Doctor pointed at the gun, which was still aimed at him. 'Tell me, Mr Tunbridge – is that gun standard issue for the maintenance team round here?'

Tunbridge smiled slyly. 'You never know who might try to sabotage the rides,' he said. 'It's best to be ready for anything.'

'I quite agree,' the Doctor said. 'But I'm not the one sabotaging the ride. And I'd be very surprised if the maintenance crew were actually issued with full-phase laser pistols, particularly as they're of a type that hasn't been invented yet here on Earth.'

Tunbridge frowned. 'You know what this is?'

'I do,' the Doctor said. 'And, judging from the way you're holding it, so do you. It isn't something you just found lying around.'

'OK, you got me,' Tunbridge admitted. 'If you know what this is, you'll also know what it can do to you. So I suggest you do exactly as I say.'

'Oh, absolutely,' the Doctor agreed.

They stood staring at each other for a few moments.

Then the Doctor added, 'So, what exactly *do* you say? Or are we just going to stand here all day until one of us gets bored and wanders off?'

Tunbridge snarled, annoyed. 'We're going to have a little chat. But not here. I've got an office not far away. You should find it quite hospitable.' He gave the Doctor a nasty grin.

'Very good,' the Doctor said. 'I like hospitable. I hope

you have some tea and biscuits. Lead the way!'

'Ha! So you can slip off while my back's turned?' Tunbridge shook his head. 'I don't think so. *You* lead the way. I'll give you directions, and I suggest you follow them precisely.'

Under Tunbridge's instruction, the Doctor descended to ground level. Prodding the gun into the Doctor's back, Tunbridge then steered them through the gloom until finally they arrived at a door.

'Open it,' Tunbridge ordered gruffly.

Beyond the door was a small office. There was a desk with a chair on either side. Tunbridge gestured for the Doctor to sit down in one chair, while he sat in the other, aiming his gun at the Doctor across the desk.

The Doctor looked around with interest. The room didn't look much like a maintenance office. There was a sophisticated-looking computer taking up one whole side of it. Shelves and racks along the other walls were covered with electronic equipment, all connected together and humming away busily. None of it was from Earth in this era.

'Tell me, where are you from?' the Doctor asked. 'I suspect, with all this equipment, that it isn't Florida – or anywhere remotely *near* Florida.'

'No. Not Florida.' Tunbridge smirked. 'But then, I don't

think you are either. In fact, I don't think you're from Earth at all.'

The Doctor smiled. 'Touché,' he said. 'Now, I don't detect any camouflage, or any perception filters, so I'd guess that you are actually humanoid. But you'll have to give me a clue as to exactly which planet you're from.'

Tunbridge didn't answer for a moment, perhaps while he decided how much to tell the Doctor.

At least he hasn't killed me yet, the Doctor thought.

'I'm from Bellcazario,' Tunbridge said at last.

'Ah, yes.' The Doctor nodded. 'Nice little place in the Umbra Constellation, if I remember rightly. What brings you all the way to Earth then?'

Based on what he had found attached to Space Plunge, the Doctor already had a good idea; but he found it was often best to play dumb to begin with.

'I'm a businessman,' Tunbridge said. 'There's a very valuable commodity here on Earth that I've been – how shall I put it? – acquiring.'

'Really?' the Doctor said, a theatrically quizzical expression on his face. 'And have you been here *acquiring* this commodity for long?'

Tunbridge frowned. 'I only started recently. So far everything has gone perfectly. Until you turned up.' He leaned

back in his chair, the gun still aimed at the Doctor. 'I'm not sure
what to do about you, Doctor.'

'Easiest just to let me go, I'd have thought,' the Doctor
said. 'I'll be on my way and you can carry on stealing the
life essence of the poor people who ride Space Plunge.' He
smiled at Tunbridge's look of surprise. 'That is what you're
doing, isn't it? I couldn't help noticing how tired everyone gets
when they leave the ride.'

'You're very clever, Doctor,' Tunbridge laughed, waving
the gun at him. 'Far too clever for my liking.'

'I get that a lot,' the Doctor replied, leaning forward to
rest his arms on the desk in front of him. 'What do you want
it for then, this life essence? You called it a commodity. Are
you selling it?'

Tunbridge sighed. 'The human race is broadly
compatible with my own – not just in terms of physical
resemblance, but in emotional and spiritual awareness too.
I'm storing the life essence I take, and when I have enough I
shall take it back to Bellcazario and sell it.'

'Is that right?'

'It certainly is.' Tunbridge smirked, seemingly starting
to enjoy explaining this all to the Doctor. 'It will have a
revitalising effect on my people. They'll pay a fortune for it!
The human life essence will help to eliminate tiredness, and

it will also add years on to my people's lives.'

'Not to mention taking years *off* the lives of the people you stole it from,' the Doctor said, his voice a low growl. 'The people you *keep* stealing it from.'

Tunbridge looked displeased. It seemed the Doctor had figured out more than he'd realized.

'I took a look at the equipment attached to the track before you found me,' the Doctor told him. 'It stores the biological signature of everyone it steals the life essence from. I imagine it uses that unique signature to keep taking it, even after they've left the ride. Am I right?'

Tunbridge frowned at the Doctor, as if wondering how much to tell him. 'Yes,' he said, after a few moments' silence.

The Doctor sat back in his chair and sighed. 'What a fine mess this is, eh? How did you even *get* here? It's too far for a transmat. You must have a ship nearby.'

Tunbridge nodded reluctantly.

'You're not worried someone might find it?'

Now Tunbridge looked smug. 'It's cloaked. And anyway, it won't be there for long, because *I* won't be here for long. My storage capacitors will shortly be full, and once they are, I can return home with my cargo. If it sells well, I might come back for more. We shall see.'

As Tunbridge spoke, the Doctor's mind was busy

working through the different ways he might be able to escape. *If I can just get away from this office*, he thought, *I think I know how to sort things out.*

'You think you'll fill your storage capacitors with life essence fairly quickly then?' he asked.

'Space Plunge is very popular,' Tunbridge told him. 'And, as you apparently already know, the passengers continue to contribute their life essence even after they have finished the ride. So, no – it won't take long at all.'

Tunbridge got up and went over to one of the pieces of alien equipment on a shelf, keeping his gun trained on the Doctor the whole time.

'See here?' He pointed to a display, with an unpleasant smirk on his face. 'This tells me how full the capacitors are. They were at over seventy per cent this morning, and now they're . . .'

Tunbridge paused to check the reading, which required him to turn away from the Doctor for just a moment. Or at least, it *should* have taken him only a moment. Instead, he stared in disbelief at the reading on the equipment. 'That can't be right,' he said. 'There must be a fault!'

'Problem?' the Doctor asked from behind him.

'It says zero,' Tunbridge said quietly, his eyes glued to the read-out. He started frantically checking the various connections on the equipment, his voice rising in panic. 'It can't be zero! The life essence can't have just drained away!'

'Not unless someone very clever rerouted the systems,' the Doctor said. 'So that, instead of being stolen from the people on the ride, the life essence was actually sent back to those it was taken from.'

'That's not possible!' Tunbridge cried. He was so focused on checking the equipment that he didn't notice the Doctor getting quietly up and moving to the door.

Now, the Doctor opened it. 'All their biological signatures were stored on the system, so I'm afraid it *is* possible,' the Time Lord said. 'Very possible indeed!'

Then he stepped quickly through the door and sonicked it shut behind him.

Tunbridge's yells of frustration faded as the Doctor ran into the gloom towards the Space Plunge tracks. His pursuer would soon be after him, and he sounded very angry. That was fine by him – angry people didn't think clearly and tended to make mistakes.

A sudden bang signalled that Tunbridge had shot the lock off the door.

The Doctor hurried on through the near-darkness, retracing the route that Tunbridge had brought him along.

He had a head start, but the question was whether he would have enough time to do what he needed to before Tunbridge caught up . . .

Finally arriving at the point on the scaffolding where he'd first met Tunbridge, the Doctor paused for a moment, listening. He couldn't hear Tunbridge, so with any luck he had a few minutes. He just hoped it would be enough time.

The Doctor took out his sonic screwdriver and set to work. He quickly disconnected the components he needed – luckily they were not especially heavy or bulky, so he stuffed them into his coat pockets, then rushed back down one of the ladders to the ground.

All he had to do now was remember where the service door was, get outside, and hunt down Tunbridge's concealed spaceship . . .

As it happened, Tunbridge wasn't far behind the Doctor at all. As soon as he'd lost his prisoner, Tunbridge had headed back to his equipment on the Space Plunge track, intending to repair whatever damage the Doctor had done. Shortly after the Doctor had disappeared down the ladder and into the gloom, Tunbridge reached the scaffolding.

He stared in horror at the mess the Doctor had left behind. Vital components had been ripped out and taken away.

It wasn't a question of repairing the damage any more – the whole system would need replacing! Tunbridge had some spare parts in his office and back on the ship, but not nearly enough for this.

Perhaps, he thought, *it would be better to call it a day and simply abandon this scheme.*

It was either that or a long journey back to Bellcazario to collect replacement components, and then all the way back to Earth again to set up the system once more. That was certainly possible, but Tunbridge had already invested a huge amount of time in this. Did he really want to waste a whole lot more? Or was he better off cutting his losses and thinking up some other way to make his fortune?

Whatever he eventually decided, his first course of action was to get back to his ship. He would have plenty of time on the way back to Bellcazario to work out if he was staying put once he got there, or whether he should come back to Earth to try again.

Once the Doctor was back outside Space Plunge, he headed for the edge of the theme park. It would make sense for Tunbridge to have left his spaceship away from the main attractions, somewhere on the perimeter of Adventure World, where the public would be unlikely to visit.

The Doctor paused to consult a map of the theme park that was mounted on a sloping plaque beside the path. *Yes, that looks like the most probable place*, he thought, touching a point on the map with a thin finger, before hurrying on.

Although Tunbridge's spaceship was cloaked, it was fairly easy to find – the Doctor knew what he was looking for, and he had a sonic screwdriver to help locate it. He quickly used the sonic to unlock the main hatch and slipped inside, hoping Tunbridge had travelled alone.

As soon as he had ascertained that the spaceship was indeed empty, the Doctor pulled the various components he had stolen from the Space Plunge track out of his pockets and sifted through them carefully. Then he began to put them together.

Once he was happy that what he had created would do what he wanted it to, he fixed it out of sight beneath the pilot's chair.

Then he let himself out of the ship and locked the main hatch behind him again.

As he made his way back towards the centre of the theme park, the Doctor thought he caught a glimpse of Tunbridge hurrying in the opposite direction. He smiled to himself, and carried on. After all the excitement of the day, he rather fancied another ice cream.

Tunbridge let himself into his ship. He closed and locked the main hatch behind him, then took his seat at the controls. Setting the flight controls to take him back to Bellcazario, he activated the autopilot.

As the ship took off, Tunbridge was pressed back into his chair by the G-force. The unpleasant sensation only lasted a few minutes, and then he was leaving Earth's gravitational field and heading back home.

I might as well get some rest, Tunbridge thought. It would be a long journey, and for some reason he suddenly felt incredibly sleepy.

Well, he supposed, *I have been rather busy for the last few weeks*.

And his encounter with that meddlesome Doctor had been particularly tiresome. He reclined the pilot's chair a little and closed his eyes.

As he began to drift off to sleep, it occurred to Tunbridge that what he was feeling was probably not unlike what the humans had experienced as he had drained their life essence. Was that a coincidence? It had to be, surely.

But then he remembered the missing components. Tunbridge thought the Doctor had taken them simply in order to stop him from repairing his equipment, but what if

there was some other purpose? *What if the Doctor . . . ?*
What if he . . . ?

Tunbridge was finding it hard to concentrate. As the
equipment the Doctor had fixed beneath Tunbridge's seat
continued to drain his life essence, Tunbridge drifted off into
a deep sleep.

It was a sleep he wouldn't wake from for a very long time.

As the Doctor turned away from the ice-cream stall, he saw a
group of people he recognised. It was the little boy, Dan, and
his parents.

They didn't look tired any more. In fact, Dan was back
to his former excitable self. He was bouncing up and down,
and running off to look at things while his parents did their
best to keep up.

Dan's mother spotted the Doctor and waved.

The Doctor wandered over to join them, licking his ice
cream before it melted too much.

'I see a bite to eat and a bit of a rest did the trick,' he
said as he reached them.

'Oh, yes,' Dan's mother said. 'I don't know why we were
suddenly so tired . . . but we're back to normal now!' She
smiled contentedly, keeping one eye on her son as he ran
happily around nearby.

'Good,' the Doctor said. 'I'm pleased.'

'Although,' Dan's father called back, as he jogged after the boy, 'if there was a way of draining off some of that boy's energy, I'd pay a fortune for it!'

The Doctor nodded and smiled. 'That's a thought,' he said. 'If only . . .'

SPECTATOR SPORT

The Doctor could smell gunpowder as soon as he stepped out of the TARDIS. In the distance, he could hear the muffled sound of cannonfire. A battle was raging somewhere nearby.

He surveyed the landscape before him. It was an especially beautiful view, with rolling green fields and a river snaking away into the distance.

Such a shame that humans are going to ruin it with cannonballs, the Doctor thought. Or he assumed they were humans. It looked as though the TARDIS had landed on Earth, but where and when precisely, the Doctor wasn't entirely sure. The old girl's calibration system was misbehaving and, until the Doctor knew his location and the date, he couldn't reset it.

Curious, he headed up a hill towards the sounds of battle. If he could see what was going on, he'd be able to get a rough idea of the date. Then he could recalibrate the TARDIS systems and be on his way.

At the top of the hill the Doctor found himself looking down into a valley. The battlefield was spread out before him, littered with bodies and dotted with puffs of smoke from guns and cannon.

A few metres away, the Doctor spotted a cannonball embedded deep in the turf. He walked over to it, then knelt down and took out his sonic screwdriver. A quick analysis told him the metal content of the cannonball – and it also confirmed what the Doctor had already worked out from the uniforms of the soldiers and the types of weaponry being used. Unless he was much mistaken, this was January 1815, and he was watching the Battle of New Orleans.

The Doctor stood up again and put away his sonic screwdriver. He shook his head sadly. So many bodies. And the fighting British and American armies didn't even know that, to all intents and purposes, the war was actually over. The Treaty of Ghent, which ended it, had been signed last month, although it wouldn't be until February that the US government ratified it. But even so . . .

Now armed with the information he needed to

recalibrate the TARDIS systems, the Doctor began to retrace his steps. But he had not gone far before he spotted a figure hurrying up the slope towards him: a rather portly woman, obviously finding the incline difficult to climb.

Although the woman was certainly dressed in a manner appropriate to the period, the Doctor's trained eye could detect a slight flickering as she moved. The approaching woman was using a perception filter – what the Doctor was seeing was not how the woman actually looked.

Intrigued, but also wary, the Doctor stopped and waited for the woman to reach him.

'There you are,' she gasped breathlessly, as she reached the Doctor.

'You were expecting me?' The Doctor wasn't quite sure what to make of this.

The woman ignored the Doctor's words. 'You really shouldn't wander away from the safe area, you know.' She paused for a moment and peered at the Doctor. 'Although, I have to confess, I don't recognise you.'

As far as the Doctor knew, they had never met before, so this was hardly surprising. But he didn't comment on it, instead raising his eyebrows and waiting for the woman – if she was a woman – to carry on.

'Anyway,' she said eventually, 'you'd better come with me

back to the safe area right away.'

'Had I?' the Doctor replied.

'Yes!' the woman insisted. 'I expect you're wondering how I found you,' she went on.

'It did cross my mind,' the Doctor agreed.

'Well, I don't know what equipment you were using, but we picked up a power emission. Any anachronism like that gets flagged, so I triangulated your position.'

The Doctor nodded. 'It must have been this,' he confessed, pulling his sonic screwdriver out of his pocket again.

'Yes, probably,' the woman agreed.

Before he put it away, the Doctor activated the sonic. He set it to disrupt the woman's perception filter, just for a couple of seconds. It wouldn't be long enough for the woman – or whatever she really was – to notice, but it would allow the Doctor to get a good look at her.

The result was rather disappointing. She still looked like a human woman. In fact, she looked exactly the same – only her clothes changed, from the early nineteenth-century frock she had been wearing, into a simple one-piece overall in an unpleasant shade of mauve.

'I'm sorry,' the woman said, not noticing that her perception filter had blinked off for a couple of seconds, 'but I don't know your name.'

'That's all right,' the Doctor said. 'I don't know yours either.'

The woman seemed surprised. 'I am Guide Mellors!'

'Of course you are,' the Doctor said. 'And you can call me the Doctor.'

Mellors frowned at this. 'Just the Doctor?'

'Just the Doctor.'

'Very well then, Doctor. We'd best be getting back to the safe area, quick.'

'I couldn't agree more,' the Doctor said, not really having any idea what Guide Mellors was talking about but intrigued none the less. 'Lead the way.'

Guide Mellors set off back down the hill, the Doctor trailing after her. They skirted round the edge of the battlefield, where there didn't seem to be any let-up in the fighting. The Doctor wondered how many more lives had been lost while he and Mellors walked casually by.

Soon, they started to ascend another hill. This one was higher than the vantage point the Doctor had reached earlier. He suspected there would be an even better view of the battlefield from the top. As they neared the summit, the Doctor thought he could detect the faintest shimmer in the air, rather like a heat haze. *Another perception filter*, he decided. Only this one was covering something huge, and masking it completely so that it was wholly invisible.

Beyond the shimmering air, there was indeed a view down to the battle. The Doctor spent a few moments staring sadly at the conflict, before he followed Mellors and stepped through the shimmer and into whatever lay beyond.

The Doctor wasn't quite sure what he had been expecting to find hidden by the perception filter, but he was surprised nevertheless. He stopped and looked up at a vast spaceship, which had been landed on top of the hill. The middle of one whole side of the ship was a huge window, and he could see a collection of people – they looked mostly humanoid from here – sipping drinks and looking down at the battle raging below them.

The Doctor didn't stay surprised for long – he never did. After a moment, he followed Guide Mellors to the main entry hatch of the ship. The Doctor waited while Mellors keyed in the entry code, and the hatch swung slowly and smoothly open. Then he followed Mellors inside, and the hatch swung closed behind them.

Inside, Mellors deactivated her perception filter and her clothes shimmered into the mauve overall the Doctor had glimpsed before.

She then led the way across a small, open area, down a short corridor and into an elevator. The doors slid shut, and the Doctor felt a slight movement as the elevator rose, taking them up to the level where people were gathered, watching the Battle of New Orleans unfold before them.

As they emerged from the elevator, Mellors picked up an electronic tablet from a side table and activated it. She spent a few moments staring at the screen, frowning. Finally, she turned to the Doctor, who raised a quizzical eyebrow.

'Problem?' the Doctor asked.

'I'm not sure,' Mellors confessed. 'But this is a list of all the people on board this tour —'

'Tour?'

'And you're not on it,' Mellors went on, ignoring the Doctor's implied question. 'There is no mention of any "Doctor" at all, so far as I can see.'

'Ah well,' the Doctor told her with a smile, 'that's easy to explain.'

'Oh?' Mellors deactivated the tablet and placed it on the table.

'I'm not on this tour of yours.'

Mellors frowned deeply. 'But you're not local.'

'True,' the Doctor agreed. 'I'm just visiting. Like you. Though I came here by accident. If you're on a tour, you must have come here deliberately.'

'Of course,' Mellors told him. 'The battles between

these primitive humans are very popular. Most tours to Earth battlefields sell out as soon as we announce them. Of course,' she went on, 'we never know quite what battle we'll find going on until we get here and scan for the use of the primitive weaponry they've developed. It's always a bit of a lottery. But this battle's been going on for a few days and is really quite spectacular!'

The Doctor was not impressed. 'You arrange tours to Earth to watch the human race wage war on itself?' he asked, a steely edge in his voice.

'Exactly.' Mellors smiled, apparently not catching the Doctor's harsh tone.

The Doctor frowned in a particularly angry manner, and Mellors finally noticed there was something wrong.

'You look as if you don't approve,' she said.

'I don't!'

'Well, we've been running these tours for decades now,' Mellors said. 'And we've never had any complaints. As I say, they're always very popular.'

'Not with me,' the Doctor growled.

'Oh well,' Mellors said lightly. 'Each to their own, I suppose. Though I can't see why you would object.'

'Object to you making war – death and destruction – a spectator sport?' the Doctor said, his voice rising. Several people over by the window turned briefly to see what the disturbance was, before going back to watching the battle and sipping their drinks. 'You really don't see *any* problem with that?' the Doctor asked incredulously.

'Honestly?' Mellors smirked. 'No, I don't. The battle will take place whether we're here or not.'

'That may be the case, but you don't have to come and glory in it!'

Mellors held up a hand in protest. 'Oh, steady on, Doctor. Battles are very interesting and give us great insight into this planet's background and way of life –'

'And way of death,' the Doctor added bitterly.

Mellors ignored him. 'But that isn't to say that we actually *condone* what's happening here.'

The Doctor scoffed. 'You don't condone it. You just come along to watch and sip cocktails! Oh,' he went on, '*and* your company makes a healthy profit from it, I assume. Profiting from the unfortunate deaths of the innocent people out there!'

'Well,' Mellors said hesitantly, 'if you put it like that, it does sound a little mercenary. But companies have to make profits, and our company is no different!'

'Forgive me if I don't agree with you, Guide Mellors,' the Doctor snarled. 'And I won't be wanting any of your drinks either, so that will save you some money.'

'Oh, are you sure?' Mellors asked jovially. 'We've a very good Caxatonian verlander that's quite popular. I have to say, it does taste magnificent.'

'No, thank you,' the Doctor snapped. 'In fact, I think I'll leave you to your "entertainment" and head back to my own ship.'

Mellors shrugged. 'As you wish.'

'I do wish,' the Doctor told her firmly. He turned back towards the lift.

But just then, something happened that changed the Doctor's mind, and shocked everyone there on the viewing deck – especially Guide Mellors. A piercing scream cut the air, echoing all around them.

It took the Doctor a moment to realise that the scream, which had been promptly followed by another, had actually come from a corridor leading off the viewing deck, close to the elevator. Mellors stood frozen, her face pale and her eyes wide. The Doctor immediately charged off down the corridor, vaguely aware that Mellors had recovered and was following him.

As the Doctor hurried down the corridor, the screams subsided to a forlorn whimpering. The corridor was lined with doors, but only one was open, and the crying was obviously coming from inside. The Doctor rushed into the room, Mellors close on his heels.

'You can't go in there!' Mellors gasped. 'That's the Throne Lord's private –' But she broke off as soon as she saw what the Doctor had already seen inside the room.

It was a luxuriously appointed suite, obviously for someone very important and influential. *Probably someone like the man lying on the bed*, the Doctor thought – or rather, sprawled across it. It was immediately obvious that the man was in a bad way.

Beside the bed stood a distraught blue-skinned woman in a waitress uniform. Her hands were covering her face and she was crying. She turned towards the doorway as the Doctor and Mellors approached.

'The Throne Lord,' Mellors murmured. 'What happened here?' she demanded of the waitress.

The waitress shook her head, struggling to speak through her sobs. 'I was bringing him a drink. When I came in there was a man – at least, I think it was a man. He pushed past me so quickly. And the Throne Lord was lying here like this . . .' Her voice trailed off and she gestured to the man lying across the bed.

As she had been speaking, the Doctor had hurried over to the man. A quick examination revealed the important details. 'He's still alive,' the Doctor said.

'Thank heavens for that,' said Mellors.

'But he's unconscious,' the Doctor went on. 'From the bruising on his neck, I'd say someone tried to strangle him.'

'But who would do that?' the waitress said.

'He's the Throne Lord of Cassakna!' Mellors cried. 'You know as well as I do that there are several other families who think they have a better claim to the title than he does. This could be the work of an agent of any one of them.' She turned to the Doctor. 'Will he be all right?'

The Doctor shrugged.

Mellors scoffed. 'You're a doctor, aren't you? You must have some idea!'

'I'm not *that* sort of doctor,' the Doctor told her. 'But I'd say he'll probably be fine. He may be unconscious for some time, and when he wakes he'll need plenty of rest. But he should make a full recovery.'

Mellors nodded thoughtfully. She turned to the waitress. 'You'd better keep this to yourself. We don't want the other tourists panicking. And if there's an assassin among us —'

'If?' The Doctor raised an eyebrow.

'All right,' Mellors agreed, 'it seems there *is* an assassin among us. So we don't want to tip off whoever it is that we know. Not until we can work out who they are, anyway.'

The waitress nodded, and sniffed away the last of her tears. 'I should get back to work,' she said quietly.

'Yes,' Mellors agreed. 'I think that's best.' She turned back to the Doctor. 'And I suppose you will be heading back to your own ship now? I would be grateful if you'd say nothing about this to any of the other tourists.'

The Doctor was still looking down at the unconscious man on the bed. 'No,' he said.

Mellors looked at him curiously. 'You mean, no, you won't say anything?'

'I mean,' the Doctor told her, looking up at last, 'no, I'm not going back to my ship. There's a would-be murderer on the loose in this so-called safe area of yours, and you'll need my help to find them.'

Not surprisingly, considering it made a habit of visiting battlegrounds, the ship had its own medical expert. Having been sworn to secrecy by Guide Mellors, Physician Krimpson examined the Throne Lord carefully.

Krimpson was an Ood doctor. The Doctor watched her closely as she made her examination – he had already decided to trust no one. Well, no one except Mellors, who had been with him when the Throne Lord was attacked.

Finally, Krimpson packed her equipment away and gave

her report. As the Doctor had already surmised, the Throne Lord was unconscious, having been starved of oxygen. But he would eventually recover. In the meantime, Krimpson advised, he should be left in peace and quiet.

'Will he remember what happened?' Mellors asked.

'Perhaps,' Krimpson said. 'Perhaps not. A traumatic experience like this might well be blanked from his memory.'

'So he may not remember who attacked him?' Mellors said.

'I'm afraid that is a distinct possibility.'

Once Krimpson had gone, Mellors and the Doctor were left alone with the unconscious Throne Lord. With Krimpson's help they had eased him into the bed and made him more comfortable.

'I have to get back to the other tourists,' Mellors said. 'Some of them will have heard the commotion, so I'd better reassure them that there's nothing wrong.'

'Even though there *is* something *very* wrong,' the Doctor said.

'Yes, Doctor,' Mellors sighed. 'I know. But the fewer people who know that, the better.'

The Doctor ignored Mellors' exasperated tone.

'Doctor . . .' Mellors paused on her way to the door. 'You said you could help us investigate who carried out this attack.'

'I did.'

'May I ask how you intend to do that?'

'Simple,' the Doctor replied. 'Whoever tried to kill the Throne Lord knows they didn't succeed.'

Mellors' eyes widened. 'You think they might try again?'

'I'm sure of it,' the Doctor told her. 'Which is why I'm going to stay here.'

'In case the assassin comes back to the scene of the crime?'

'To finish the job,' the Doctor said. 'Exactly. I'm not part of your tour, so whoever it is won't know I'm on the ship. Even if the assassin checks where everyone is, to make sure they won't be disturbed when they make their second attempt on this man's life, they won't have a clue that I'll be waiting for them.'

Mellors nodded. 'It's a clever plan, certainly.' She paused as she reached the doorway. 'But, for heaven's sake, Doctor – do be careful.'

'I always am,' the Doctor replied.

'The culprit is a killer. A cold-blooded killer.'

The Doctor glanced at the unconscious Throne Lord. 'I know that,' he said. 'Don't worry. I've dealt with a lot of cold-blooded killers in my time.'

Mellors stared back at the Doctor for a moment, then

she nodded again. 'Yes,' she said quietly. 'Yes, I can believe that you have.' Then she stepped out into the corridor, closing the door behind her.

The Doctor stood for a while, not moving. He was thinking through his options. If the killer returned – or rather *when* the killer returned, as the Doctor was sure they would – they would have to come in through the same door Mellors had just left by. The only other door in the room led into a small bathroom.

The Doctor made a quick tour of the room, sizing up the crime scene – there was the bed, complete with its unconscious occupant, and a large area evidently meant for relaxing. There were several armchairs, a small sofa, and rugs on the floor with intricate designs woven into them.

After careful consideration, the Doctor repositioned one of the armchairs and sat in it. Yes, this was perfect. From here he could see the Throne Lord in the bed and had a good view of the door. Whoever came in through the door would see the bed first, and probably not realise there was anyone else in the room as they made for their prey.

Satisfied, the Doctor leaned back in the chair and waited.

After a while, he began to wonder if he had been correct. What if the assassin did not come back? What if they'd already fled? How long should he wait here to see if anything happened? *I'll wait until the Throne Lord regains consciousness*, he decided. Then he could check the man was all right and be on his way.

It was strange, the Doctor thought – the possible death of this one man here in the room with him seemed so much more immediate than the deaths of all the British and American soldiers in the battle outside. But then, he reminded himself, the soldiers' deaths were already recorded in history. The Doctor couldn't change that. Here, however, he had a chance to save a life. Whether the Throne Lord's life was actually worth saving or not, the Doctor had no idea. Was the man a good ruler, or a tyrant? Not that it mattered. A life was a life, and murder was still murder whoever the victim might be.

The Doctor let his mind drift off into memories of times and places he had been, and thoughts of times and places he would like to visit. He was jolted out of his reverie as the door slowly opened.

A tall, broad man had slipped into the room. He closed the door quietly behind him and turned towards the bed. His attention was completely focused on the unconscious Throne Lord, and he failed to notice the Doctor watching him.

The Doctor waited. After all, this might just be someone checking on the Throne Lord. A medic, sent by Krimpson perhaps. *Or perhaps not*, the Doctor thought, as the man walked over to the bed, and reached for the Throne Lord's throat.

The Doctor cleared his own throat loudly. The man jerked upright and turned quickly towards him.

'I thought you'd be back,' the Doctor said. 'Come to finish the job, have you?' He smiled. 'I'm the Doctor, by the way. Didn't catch your name.'

The man regarded the Doctor thoughtfully. For a while he was silent. When he did speak, his voice was deep and mellow.

'You have seen me,' he said.

'Yes, I certainly have,' the Doctor confirmed.

'There must be no witnesses,' the man told him, walking slowly towards the Doctor.

The Doctor stood up. It occurred to him that he should have arranged with Mellors to have some sort of communicator so he could call for help when the assassin returned. *A bit late for that now*, he thought. He stared back at the man. There was something odd about him, the Doctor thought – and not just that he was a killer. It was the smooth way he moved. The lack of any depth to his eyes . . . It was obvious that the man was going to try to kill him.

If I can get to the door, the Doctor thought, *he might well follow me and leave the Throne Lord.* There was just one problem with that: the assassin was now between the Doctor and the door. The Doctor looked around for something that might help. Glancing down, he saw what to do.

The man hesitated as the Doctor smiled. The approaching killer didn't pause for long – but it was long enough for the Doctor to bend down and quickly grab the edge of the ornate rug the man was standing on. The Doctor heaved as hard as he could, yanking the rug out from under the man's feet.

As the Doctor had hoped, the man was thrown off balance. With a cry of surprise, he crashed to the floor, and his head smashed into a low table. He landed face down, and lay still, close to the Doctor's feet.

The Doctor stood and looked down at the man for a moment. He was about to step over the man – who he assumed was knocked unconscious – to go and find Guide Mellors, when the assassin rolled on to his back and stared up at him.

Except it was now apparent that this wasn't a man at all.

Where his head had hit the table, the skin had been gouged away to reveal what was beneath, and it wasn't flesh and bone any more than the skin was really skin. It was metal. Lights flickered, and the Doctor detected the almost silent movement of gears as the man's – or rather the robot's – lips twitched and it spoke.

'It isn't that easy to stop me,' the robot said, pulling itself back to its feet.

It only took the robot a few moments to get up, but it was long enough for the Doctor to slip past it and get to the door. He paused for long enough to be sure the robot was coming after him instead of returning to the Throne Lord, then ran off down the corridor.

The Doctor didn't head for the viewing deck. Goodness only knew what this automaton would do if confronted with a crowd of tourists; it might well slaughter them all. Instead, the Doctor headed the other way, deeper into the ship.

He didn't need to look back to know the robot was coming after him; he could hear its heavy feet reverberating on the metal floor. As he ran, the Doctor hoped that what he assumed about the design of the ship was actually correct. He raced past more closed doors, then into an open area with several corridors leading off it.

After a brief hesitation, the Doctor picked the corridor most likely to head where he wanted to go, and ran on. The robot was gaining on him, he was sure of it. But if he could just keep ahead of it until they reached the end of the corridor . . .

The Doctor saw with relief another elevator appear at
the end of the hallway. If his guess had indeed been correct,
this elevator would lead down into the hold of the ship. Now
the Doctor just had to hope the elevator was already at this
floor. If he had to wait, the robot would catch up with him –
and that would be the end of the Doctor.

Unless, the Doctor realised, *I call the elevator now*.

He fumbled in his pocket and found his sonic
screwdriver. With luck, he could simulate the ultrasound pulse
that called the elevator in this class of ship. He managed to
adjust the settings as he ran, and triggered the pulse.

Sure enough, just as he reached the end of the corridor
– the robot not far behind him now – the elevator doors
slid smoothly open. The Doctor dived inside and pressed
the button that would take the elevator down to the hold.
The doors slid shut just as the robot reached them. The
Doctor heard a loud clang as the robot's fist thumped the
closed doors, but it was too late. The elevator was already
descending.

Now the Doctor had to work out how he was going to
deal with the robot when it followed him down to the hold.
His first priority, he decided, was to get it away from the ship
so it couldn't harm the Throne Lord or anyone else
on board.

So, rather than heading straight for the exit hatch when he stepped out of the elevator and into the hold of the ship, the Doctor waited. He needed to make sure that the robot saw him and followed. How he would deal with it once they were outside the ship, the Doctor had no idea – but he'd worry about that in a minute.

The elevator was already heading back up in response to the robot pressing the call button. The Doctor wouldn't have to wait long. He went over to the exit hatch and opened it, keying in the code he had seen Guide Mellors use when they had arrived at the ship. As soon as the robot saw him, he could duck outside and close the hatch. That would buy him a little time, at least.

The elevator doors slid open again and the robot stepped out. It turned slowly, surveying the area, and the light glinted on the metal beneath the torn skin of its face.

The Doctor raised his arm, hoping the movement would draw the robot's attention. It did. The automaton turned towards the Doctor, then started quickly across the hold.

The Doctor leapt through the hatch and pressed the close button on the other side. He looked around to get his bearings. He was in a field on the top of the hill. There was very little cover. Looking down the hill, he could see a small wooded area, and beyond that the two armies fighting each

other. Not far away, a line of cannon was letting off shots.
The air was full of smoke and the smell of gunpowder.

Behind the Doctor, the hatch slid open again. With no
more time to think, the Doctor set off at a run. He headed
down the hill – towards the battle. A glance back over his
shoulder was enough to tell him that the robot was following.
And, unlike the Doctor, the robot would not eventually tire
and need rest. Unless the Doctor came up with a plan fairly
soon, the robot would catch him. And when that happened . . .

The small wooded area was off to the right, and the
Doctor set off towards it. He might buy himself some thinking
time by hiding among the trees. As he reached the treeline he
was still a good way ahead of the robot.

He headed for the deepest and darkest part of the wood.
The canopy of trees masked the sunlight so that the whole
area was dim and gloomy.

Hiding behind one particularly large tree trunk, the
Doctor could hear the robot moving through the wood,
searching for him. Branches broke beneath the robot's feet as
it tramped onwards. It would find him eventually, the Doctor
knew. Now, though, the Doctor had an idea for how to deal
with the thing. The only problem was getting the idea to work.

He risked looking out from behind the tree to see where
the robot was. A mistake: although the robot was a good way

off, it spotted the Doctor immediately.

There was no option but to run for it. Again.

The Doctor set off through the wood, the robot in pursuit. He had a half-formed plan in his mind as he pushed his way through the maze of branches and leaves.

The Doctor burst out of the trees and found himself back on open ground. The noise of the battle was much louder here, and he saw that he was much closer to it. In fact, he was actually on the edge of the battlefield. A cannonball flew past him and buried itself in the ground not fifteen metres from where he was standing. Strangely, the Doctor smiled. The last details of his plan clicked into place.

He looked out across the battle, noting the positions of the cannon and the directions in which they were aimed. He watched the soldiers yelling at each other, firing their rifles. And he turned to see the robot emerge from the woods and head straight for him.

His timing, the Doctor knew, would have to be perfect, as would the positioning. There was also a large amount of luck involved. But, despite the danger and the huge number of things that could go wrong, the Doctor stood his ground. He waited for the robot to approach, a slight smile still on his face.

The robot stopped in front of the Doctor. 'And now,' it said levelly, 'you die.'

'That may be *your* plan,' the Doctor responded. 'But it certainly isn't mine.'

Behind his back, he had his fingers crossed. A short distance away on the battlefield, he noted the puff of smoke as a cannon fired. The Doctor watched the progress of the cannonball through the air. It was so fast it was little more than a blur, but his mind was racing through calculations of velocity and angle.

Then he ran.

Immediately the robot gave chase.

When the Doctor reached what he hoped was the exact spot where he needed to be, he suddenly stopped. The smoking cannonball that had flown past the Doctor earlier was lying just a couple of metres away. Well, that was a good sign.

The Doctor turned as the robot gained on him. It hesitated, obviously uncertain as to why the Doctor had stopped. It regarded him warily, head tilted slightly to one side.

'Yes,' the Doctor said. 'Exactly there, I think.'

The robot opened its mouth to speak, but it never got the chance. The cannonball that the Doctor had been watching soar through the air slammed down into the robot's back. It knocked the automaton to the ground and smashed right through its body. The robot exploded, and the Doctor stepped back smartly to avoid the shower of sparks and debris that spewed out of the machine.

All that was left now was a smoking mess in the rough shape of a man. The Doctor walked slowly over to the sputtering wreckage.

'Well,' he said quietly, 'that ought to do it.' He bent down to take a closer look.

Satisfied that there was not enough of the robot left for anyone to find anything anachronistic, the Doctor straightened up and looked around. He needed to get off the battlefield as quickly as possible, before a cannonball flattened him as well.

Making his way quickly back to the safety of the woods, the Doctor thought grimly that the Throne Lord and the rest of the passengers were safe – at least for now. He would send a message to Guide Mellors from the TARDIS, rather than return in person. The Doctor didn't approve of the idea of making war a spectator sport, but he doubted he could get any of them to change their minds. No – now that the robot was destroyed and the danger to the tourists had been dealt with, he'd do better to get back to his ship and be on his way.

The Doctor paused to look back across the battlefield once more. War really was a terrible thing. This battle, so far as history was concerned, had already happened. The Doctor couldn't change that. But there were other battles, other wars and conflicts, that the Doctor could help to ensure never happened in the first place. And the sooner he got back to the TARDIS, the sooner he could start.

He turned and walked away, leaving the sound of cannonfire and the smell of gunpowder behind him.

BASE OF
OPERATIONS

It really is most peculiar, the Doctor thought. He made the TARDIS check the readings again, but there was no mistake. Someone was using a transmat system somewhere nearby.

'This is the USA in May 1944,' the Doctor said aloud to himself, 'so that definitely should *not* be happening.'

Determined to get to the bottom of things, the Doctor ran from the TARDIS console room through to a smaller storeroom with an ancient-looking cupboard in the corner. He rummaged frantically through old yo-yos, spare shoes, umbrellas, and various electrical bits and pieces before he at last unearthed what it was that he was looking for. Smiling, he stuffed a small, portable emissions detector into his pocket. If he could get the TARDIS to land close to the signal he had

picked up, then he would be able to use the handheld device
to pinpoint the origin of the rogue transmat and find out who
was operating it.

He returned to the console room and plugged the flight
coordinates into the detection systems. A few moments
later, the TARDIS dematerialised, then almost instantly
rematerialised. The Doctor checked the readings, pleased to
see that he had landed very close to the emission source. But,
when he opened the scanner, the view it showed was distinctly
disappointing: a high, chain-link fence with barbed wire at
the top.

Well, the Doctor thought, *there has to be a way through the
fence somewhere . . .*

Upon stepping out of the TARDIS, the Doctor
discovered a bright, sunny day. He strolled slowly alongside
the chain-link fence. Peering through it, he saw rows of trucks
painted in camouflage colours, and the sort of one-storey,
functional buildings that the military so often utilised. He was
at the edge of an army base.

Hardly surprising, the Doctor thought. *Looks like a staging
post. Most likely, troops are being assembled here before they're shipped
over to England for the D-Day landings next month.*

Not that he would mention that to anyone. If anyone
caught whiff of the fact that he knew about the top-secret

invasion of Normandy that was planned, they'd probably decide he was a spy and shoot him.

The Doctor spotted the main entrance to the base ahead of him, the gates heavily guarded. He checked his emissions detector. No doubt about it – whoever was operating the transmat system was somewhere inside the army base. So, now more intrigued than ever, the Doctor walked up to the main gate.

'Who's the commanding officer on this base?' the Doctor asked firmly, before the guard on the gate could say anything.

'Who's asking?' the guard demanded warily.

'I'm here on orders from General Eisenhower,' the Doctor said, pulling his psychic paper from his pocket and waving it in front of the guard's face. 'Routine inspection to check everything's progressing as it should. Now, are you going to answer my question?'

The guard snapped to attention as the Doctor returned the psychic paper to his pocket. 'General Heyman is in command, sir.'

The Doctor nodded as if this was precisely what he had expected. 'And where can I find General Heyman?'

The guard gave the Doctor directions to the general's office. The Doctor thanked him, and walked through the gate into the army base.

On his way to the general's office, the Doctor passed several soldiers. He had no idea how many men were currently stationed here, but it looked like several hundred at least. The base was huge. Most of the soldiers he saw were unremarkable, but one of them walked stiffly by in a manner that made the Doctor stop and watch. He couldn't quite put his finger on what it was, but he had a sudden feeling that something was wrong. The man's body language, the way he carried himself – it just didn't seem right.

The Doctor frowned, then continued on his way to a long building with a sign outside reading: COMMAND POST.

Mounting a few steps and opening the door, the Doctor entered the building and found himself in a small outer office. A nameplate on the desk identified the man sitting behind it as Colonel Preston. The man looked up in surprise as the Doctor entered. He was young for a colonel, and had short dark hair.

The Doctor had his psychic paper out again before Colonel Preston could say a word.

'General Eisenhower sent me,' the Doctor said, flashing the psychic paper at Preston. 'Here to check everything's on schedule. So,' he went on quickly, 'I'd like a word with General Heyman as soon as possible.'

If Preston was at all taken off guard, he hid it well.

He stood up and gestured to a chair on the other side of the desk. 'Of course, sir. If you'll just take a seat, I'll see if the general is free to see you.'

'Thank you.'

As the Doctor sat down, Preston went over and knocked sharply on a door that clearly led into the general's office. After a short moment, Preston disappeared through the door.

Left alone, the Doctor checked the emissions detector again. The source of the emissions was definitely nearby.

If I can get General Heyman to organise a tour of the base, the Doctor thought, *then I should be able to find the rogue transmat and discover who's behind it.*

After a few moments, Colonel Preston returned, his jaw set as though he was determined not to give away his thoughts. 'General Heyman says he hasn't been informed of any inspection – not from General Eisenhower or from anyone else.'

'It's a surprise visit,' the Doctor told him with a smile. 'Ike likes to keep everyone on their toes.'

Colonel Preston considered this for a moment. 'I see,' he said. 'Well then, the general will see you. If you'd like to go through?'

The Doctor didn't bother knocking; he walked briskly straight into the general's office. The room was dominated by an enormous desk, and sitting behind it was an equally enormous man. General Heyman wasn't especially overweight, but he was broad and thick-set. He stood up as the Doctor entered, reaching out his hand. He was a good six inches taller than the Doctor.

There is something distinctly odd about General Heyman's grip, the Doctor thought as they shook hands. The man's palm was clammy, and his grip nowhere near as strong as the Doctor would have expected from such a large man, particularly one in a position of authority. He sat down in the chair opposite the general.

'So, what can I do for you?' General Heyman asked, also sitting back down. 'Or rather, for General Eisenhower?'

'I need to inspect the base,' the Doctor said. 'Eisenhower is keen to know that everything's on schedule and going according to plan.' As he spoke, and without looking down, the Doctor held the emissions detector under the desk, then activated it.

'It is,' General Heyman replied. 'But you're welcome to take a look for yourself.'

'Thank you.' The Doctor pointed to a door he had spotted at the back of the room, behind the general's desk. 'What's through there?' he asked.

Heyman turned to glance in the direction the Doctor was

pointing. 'Oh, that's just a storeroom,' he said dismissively.

'Can I take a look?' the Doctor asked.

'No,' the general replied curtly. He paused, then smiled. 'As I said, it's just a storeroom. There's nothing at all of interest to see through there.'

'OK.' The Doctor nodded. 'If you say so.'

Actually, the Doctor suspected there *was* a good deal of interest to see in the storeroom, but there was something else he wanted to check first. He changed the calibration on his emissions detector, and the device indicated a cloaking system operating just a few metres away. On the other side of the desk, in fact. Exactly where General Heyman was sitting.

Whoever – or whatever – was sitting in the general's chair was certainly not General Heyman. Almost certainly, it was not human at all.

The Doctor said nothing, hiding this new discovery from the man opposite him. Before he gave anything away, he needed to ascertain if whoever – or whatever – it was that was posing as Heyman was alone, or if there were others like him on the base.

Heyman was busy offering to arrange for the Doctor to have a look around the base.

'That's very kind,' the Doctor said. He could do with the help of someone in authority if he was going to find out what was happening here. 'I imagine you're far too busy yourself. Perhaps Colonel Preston could show me around?' he suggested.

'Fine,' Heyman agreed. 'The colonel can do the honours.'

It's possible Colonel Preston resented being asked to escort the Doctor around the base without any notice, but it seemed he was professional enough not to show it. As he led the Doctor outside, he asked what it was he wanted to see, exactly.

'Everything,' the Doctor told him, gesticulating at the whole army base.

'All right,' Preston said. 'We'll start with the canteen, as it's just over there. Then we'll go on to the barracks.'

As they walked, the Doctor checked the small emissions detector yet again. No cloaking emission from Preston; at least the colonel was human. If and when the Doctor needed an ally, Preston was probably a sound choice.

Although he would have liked to have done more checking, the Doctor didn't want to arouse suspicion and slid the detector back into his pocket. As they walked towards the canteen, they passed several soldiers who, much like the one the Doctor had seen on his way to the general's office, just didn't seem right. Something about the way they stood or walked or watched him struck him as wrong.

It's as if they aren't really human at all, the Doctor thought.

It wasn't mealtime, so the canteen was completely empty. A cook and several other staff were working in the kitchens out the back. They spared the Doctor and Colonel Preston little more than a glance as they conducted their inspection. The Doctor subtly checked his detector again, but it revealed nothing untoward.

The barracks, however, was a different matter. There were soldiers lying on their beds, or tidying things away. Others were polishing boots, oiling rifles or tending to their kit. The Doctor surreptitiously checked his device, and this time it picked up several emissions.

This is not an infiltration by a lone alien, the Doctor concluded. *It's an invasion waiting to happen.*

Next stop was the weapons store. The Doctor looked around at the various tools of destruction, doing his best to hide his disgust.

'What's that?' he asked, pointing to a large square metal object with a dial set in the side.

'It's a bomb,' Preston told him. 'A big one. We call it a bridge-buster, for obvious reasons.'

'Complete with timer, I see,' the Doctor said, examining the dial. 'I guess you'd want enough time to get far away before this thing went off.'

'You certainly would,' Preston confirmed.

Once they'd looked at the parade ground and the motor pool, the Doctor assured Colonel Preston that he had seen enough.

'I think it's time I have another little chat with General Heyman,' the Doctor said.

Once they were back at the general's office, Preston again asked the Doctor to wait while he checked if General Heyman was free to see him. It wasn't long before the Doctor was ushered back in to the office, and taking his seat on the opposite side of General Heyman's desk.

'So,' the general asked, 'did you see everything you needed to?'

'I think so,' the Doctor said. 'Though I would like to know what you're up to.'

General Heyman frowned. 'We're preparing the troops ready to be shipped out to Britain.'

'Oh, I didn't mean the military,' the Doctor said. 'I know what the humans' plans are.'

'The humans?' Heyman raised a suspicious eyebrow.

'That's right,' the Doctor told him. 'I want to know *your* plans, whoever – or whatever – you are.'

'I'm General Michael Heyman,' the general replied coolly.

'Yes, you look just like him, I'm sure,' the Doctor said. 'But you're not really him, are you? Come on, you can stop pretending. In fact –' the Doctor took out his sonic screwdriver – 'why don't I make it easier for you?'

The Doctor activated the sonic screwdriver, and Heyman snarled in disbelief as his human form shimmered and slowly changed. Before the Doctor's eyes, the broad-shouldered general transformed into a vast reptilian creature with shiny black scales and bloodshot yellow eyes – an enormous, angry alien lizard.

'That is not contemporary human technology,' the creature rasped, pointing a clawed finger at the Doctor's sonic screwdriver.

'No,' the Doctor admitted, putting the sonic back in his pocket, 'it's not. But then I'm neither contemporary nor human.'

'Who are you?' the creature snarled.

'I'm just a visitor,' the Doctor assured it. 'I drop in on planet Earth from time to time. What's your excuse?'

There was a loud click from behind the Doctor, and he glanced back over his shoulder. There was nothing to see, but he was pretty sure that the door had just locked, trapping him in here with the reptilian creature.

'I am Reginta of the Valbrect race,' the creature told the

Doctor. 'And, since you will not leave this room alive, I will tell you what you want to know.'

'Wonderful. You can start by telling me why you're here,' the Doctor said. His mind was already racing through possible escape routes.

'To conquer this pathetic little world,' Reginta said. 'It is rich in minerals and ores that are valuable to the Valbrects. Soon we shall make this planet ours and turn humankind into our slaves.'

'Oh, really?' The Doctor was unimpressed. 'Well, you're not the first to make that claim – or the last, come to that. But I suspect you'll need more than just the few of you disguised as humans here on this base. Oh, yes,' he went on with a smile, 'I know you haven't come here alone.'

'This is just the beginning,' Reginta snapped back. 'We shall soon have Valbrect agents stationed everywhere significant on Earth. Eventually, all the US troops will be replaced with Valbrects, and once we have control of the military we'll seize control of the planet.'

'I suppose that might work,' the Doctor conceded. 'It's certainly bold, I'll give you that. But the humans will fight back, and I imagine in your guise as General Heyman you've got quite a good idea of what they are capable of.'

The lizard creature nodded its scaly head. 'I have. But it

is of no consequence. We shall triumph easily.'

'What makes you so sure?' the Doctor asked.

'Our timing is perfect,' the creature replied. 'The human race is tearing itself apart in a global conflict. The longer we can make this war last, the weaker and more vulnerable the humans will become. When they are at their weakest, we shall strike.'

'I see,' the Doctor said. 'Yes, very clever. Although, this is 1944, and the war may not go on as long as you hope.'

'You cannot possibly know how long this war will last,' the lizard creature told him.

The Doctor smiled, but said nothing. Of course, he knew the war would end in September the following year, but there was no advantage in telling the creature that.

'So where are the humans you replaced?' the Doctor asked instead. 'Have you killed them?'

The creature gave a cruel laugh. 'No. We do not waste valuable resources. Humans make good slaves. And, in any case, we need their bodies alive so we can replicate them.'

'Ah.' The Doctor nodded. 'A bit like Zygon body prints.'

'Like what?' But before the Doctor could respond the creature waved a scaly hand. 'No matter. The humans are being held in stasis on our mothership. Once the world has been subjugated, they will be woken and will join the other human slaves, to mine this world's minerals for us.'

'I doubt it will come to that,' the Doctor said quietly.

'You know nothing,' the alien lizard spat. 'And in a few moments you will be dead, so your opinion hardly matters anyway.'

'Well, whether you value my opinion or not,' the Doctor said, 'I have to tell you that I think you're wrong on almost all the important points there.' He counted them off on his fingers as he spoke. 'I don't think your invasion will work. The human race will never be your slaves. And I have no intention of dying just yet.'

The terrifying lizard creature stood up suddenly, knocking its chair over with a clatter, and banged its claws on the desk. 'You really think you have any *choice* in the matter?' It laughed.

But Reginta could not see that the Doctor was holding his sonic screwdriver inside his jacket pocket. Hoping he'd managed to set it correctly, the Doctor activated it. He was relieved to hear a loud click behind him. The door was unlocked again. Realising he had only seconds to escape, the Doctor leapt out of his chair and ran for the door.

The creature's snorts of laughter turned swiftly into a bellow of rage, as the Doctor threw open the door and disappeared into the outer office.

Colonel Preston looked up from his work at his desk as the Doctor slammed the door to the general's office shut behind him. 'Are you done, sir?' he asked.

The Doctor fixed him with a stern stare. 'Oh, I've only just started!'

The door to the general's office opened again. The Doctor whirled round to find General Heyman standing in the doorway. The creature had reactivated its cloaking device.

'Colonel,' General Heyman – or rather, Reginta – said, 'this man is a spy. Place him under arrest immediately.'

'Don't listen to him,' the Doctor said evenly.

'Colonel, you have your orders,' Heyman said with annoyance. 'Now, arrest this man. Immediatcly!'

'You don't have to do what he tells you,' the Doctor said as Preston approached with handcuffs at the ready. 'He's not your commanding officer.'

Preston hesitated. 'What do you mean?'

'I mean that is *not* General Heyman. Look!' The Doctor activated his sonic screwdriver again, and General Heyman's body shimmered and morphed into the enormous black lizard creature.

'What the –' Preston gasped.

'Don't just stand there,' the Doctor told him. 'Run!'

Preston did not need any further encouragement. He and the Doctor rushed across the small office and out of the main door. The Doctor slammed it behind them and sonicked it shut.

'What *is* that thing?' Preston asked, looking horrified. 'And what has it done with the general?'

'It's called a Valbrect,' the Doctor said, 'and it's kidnapped your general, along with a number of your men.'

'What?' Preston looked incredulous. 'There are *more* of those things?'

'I'm not sure how many of them there are exactly,' the Doctor said. 'But I do know that several others have infiltrated your troops. Like the general in there, they're disguised as ordinary soldiers. And, if we don't do something about it, they will take control of your planet.'

Preston breathed out heavily. It was a lot to take in. 'So how do we stop them?' he asked. 'I mean, we don't even know which soldiers are human, do we?'

'Not yet,' the Doctor confirmed. He held up his sonic screwdriver. 'But if I make a few adjustments I think I can arrange it so that, once their cloaking devices – their disguises – are turned off, they can't turn them back on again.'

'So we'll know who they are,' Preston said. 'But *then* what do we do about them?'

'You're the soldier,' the Doctor said, 'and you're being invaded. I'd have thought that was more your area of expertise than mine, to be honest.'

'Right,' Preston agreed, his thoughts scrambling to form a plan.

The Doctor adjusted the settings on his sonic screwdriver. 'OK,' he said. 'When I activate this, the aliens' true nature will be revealed.' He held the sonic aloft. 'I hope your men can cope with the surprise.'

'I hope so too, Dr Smith,' Colonel Preston said grimly.

The Doctor activated the sonic screwdriver.

For a few moments it seemed as though nothing had happened. But then shouts of alarm erupted all around them. Soldiers ran out of buildings, pointing and shouting.

'It's up to you now, Colonel,' the Doctor said, slipping his sonic screwdriver back into his pocket. 'If you can keep the other Valbrects contained on the base, I will try to get back into the general's office and find a solution.'

'Good luck, Doctor,' Preston said. 'I won't let you down.' He hurried over to the nearest group of soldiers, already shouting orders at them.

As he ran back to the general's office, the Doctor saw several lizard creatures emerging from various buildings.

They're probably as confused as the human soldiers, the Doctor thought.

They would have no idea at all why their camouflage had suddenly stopped working, and their natural instinct would be to group together – which suited the Doctor perfectly.

Sure enough, the lizards all made for the same point at the corner of one of the barracks blocks. Now all he needed was for Reginta to come out of his office and join them. With luck, he'd want to take charge of the situation.

The Doctor hid beside the general's office and waited. Before long, the door opened, and Reginta emerged. He stood for a moment on the steps, looking across at the other Valbrects, then he hurried off to join them.

As soon as Reginta was on his way, the Doctor slipped behind him and through the door. He quickly made his way past Colonel Preston's desk and into the general's office. Behind him, he could already hear the rattle of gunfire. Pretty soon, he knew, it would be a pitched battle out there. He just hoped that what he was planning would work – and that he could get it to work before anyone was killed.

The Doctor walked quickly over to the storeroom door. It was locked, but the Doctor opened it easily with his sonic screwdriver. He pulled it open, and stared at the mass of equipment inside.

'Well well,' he muttered under his breath. 'That's definitely a transmat system.'

He set to work.

Outside, Colonel Preston had managed to organise his men. There were about twenty of the Valbrects in total. Several of the creatures had rifles, and were firing back at the troops, and even those that weren't armed were still extremely dangerous. Preston watched in horror as a Valbrect slashed at a soldier who got too close to its sabre-like claws. Bullets didn't seem to have any effect on the aliens, either; they just ricocheted off their scaly skin as if it was armour.

The only good news was that Preston didn't have to organise multiple battles, since the creatures seemed to be staying close together as they made their way through the base. He wasn't sure if the troops had actually killed any of the creatures, though, because the smoke drifting across the base obscured his view.

Whatever Dr Smith is planning, Preston thought, *he'd better get on with it.*

He didn't fancy the idea of a horde of enormous lizards breaking out of his base. Preston was under no illusion that if they got close enough to any civilians they wouldn't tear them apart with their claws.

✹

The Doctor had detached various components from the transmat. It took him a few minutes, but he'd eventually found what he was looking for: the bio-scanner array. This was the part of the system that identified the life form being transmatted and made sure that it was properly assembled again when it appeared at the other end.

He just hoped he could adjust it so that it would do what he wanted it to when he operated the main transmat systems. Stepping back moments later, he surveyed his handiwork. He reckoned he'd done it. He carefully reassembled the system and put away his sonic screwdriver. Now all he had to do was press the activation button.

But, before he had a chance, a large shadow fell across him. Turning abruptly, the Doctor found the huge, scaly form of Reginta towering above him in the doorway.

'What are you doing?' the lizard demanded.

'Oh, nothing much,' the Doctor said. 'Just having a bit of a tinker. You're not out there commanding your troops – I mean your lizard troops.'

'The humans are no match for my soldiers,' Reginta said. 'I can leave them to it. Now I shall return to the mothership.'

'Running away?' the Doctor said. 'Very wise. Get out while you still can.'

'I am going to fetch reinforcements,' the lizard rasped. 'Once this puny show of force has been neutralised, we shall proceed with our invasion plan.'

'I don't think so,' the Doctor said.

'You know nothing,' the lizard told him. 'I shall return with an army and crush these pathetic humans.'

'Not from here you won't,' the Doctor said. 'I'm afraid I changed things around a little while you were out.'

The creature stared past the Doctor at the transmat equipment. 'What have you done?' it asked suspiciously.

'Well,' the Doctor said, 'you're obviously interested, so I'll show you.'

He pressed the activation button.

Nothing happened at first, and the Doctor wondered if perhaps he'd made a mistake.

Then the lizard in front of him faded away.

A split-second later another figure materialised in the lizard's place. The real General Heyman stood, staring in astonishment at the Doctor.

'Who are you?' the general demanded. He looked around. 'And how the devil did I get back here?'

'Long story,' the Doctor told him. 'I've no time to explain

right now, because I just have to check something.'

He pushed past the confused general, and hurried across his office and out of the door. Once outside, he spotted Colonel Preston and his men looking in surprise at a group of soldiers, who were standing at the corner of one of the buildings. The soldiers looked rather surprised themselves.

'What happened?' Preston asked as the Doctor joined him.

'I adjusted the transmat's bio-scanner array to scan for Valbrects down here on the base, and for humans on their ship,' the Doctor said. 'I won't bore you with the details but, basically, I swapped the real soldiers for the imposters.'

'So is that it?' Colonel Preston asked. 'Are we safe now?'

'Not quite yet,' the Doctor confessed. 'I'm afraid there's nothing to stop them from coming back. Now I know that you're all safe here, I need to go to their ship. I want a word with the Valbrects.'

'A word?' Preston frowned. 'You're sure you can reason with those creatures, Dr Smith?'

The Doctor shrugged. 'I won't know until I try. But I need to make sure they go away and don't come back.'

Preston nodded. 'How can I help?'

'You can have a word with General Heyman – the real General Heyman, that is. I think he might be a little confused.'

'He's not the only one,' Preston said.

'And there's something I need from your armaments store,' the Doctor added. 'A bargaining chip that I hope I won't have to use.' The Doctor explained what he wanted, then gave the colonel a cheery pat on the back. 'I'll see you in the general's office shortly.'

The Doctor hurried back to the storeroom and set to work adjusting the transmat so that it would work normally again. It didn't take him long to fix, and shortly afterwards Colonel Preston and his men arrived.

'Is this what you wanted, sir?' Preston asked, pointing to the large object his men had just carried in to the general's office.

'It is,' the Doctor replied. 'Carry it through here for me, please.' He held the storeroom door open for them.

The soldiers set the heavy bridge-buster bomb down on the transmat pad.

The Doctor activated the transmat, and the soldiers and Colonel Preston watched in astonishment as the bomb faded away.

High above planet Earth, Reginta and the other Valbrects working at various control consoles also watched in amazement as the bomb suddenly appeared on the bridge of their mothership.

Reginta moved over to inspect it, but before he even got very close he realised what it must be.

The transmat whirred into life again, and this time a tall, wiry figure appeared. It was the Doctor.

'You!' Reginta hissed, glaring at the Time Lord. 'You dare to come here after what you have done?'

'Upset your plans a bit, have I?' the Doctor asked cheerily. 'Well, I'm here to upset them a bit more. Or, at least, I'm going to offer you a deal.'

'A deal?' Reginta looked around at the other lizards; they were all paying rapt attention to what was going on. 'What makes you think we would deal with a primitive like you?'

'I'm hardly primitive,' the Doctor protested. 'I could have set this to explode as soon as it arrived on your ship,' he continued, gesturing at the bomb, 'but I'm a generous man, so I'm giving you a chance to do what I ask. Go away now. Leave this planet in peace.'

'And why would we do that?' Reginta demanded.

'If you do,' the Doctor said, 'I won't blow up your ship, and everyone gets to live. That's a pretty good deal, I'd say.'

'We are the Valbrect,' Reginta snorted. 'We take orders from no one.'

'Last chance,' the Doctor said calmly. 'Stay and die, or leave and live. It's up to you.'

Reginta considered this, while the other lizard creatures muttered among themselves.

'And if you ever do come back,' the Doctor added, 'then rest assured: I will be waiting for you. Tell your people that planet Earth is defended. You can find your minerals and ores somewhere else.' The Doctor raised his sonic screwdriver. 'I'll leave the bomb with you,' he said. 'If you're not out of range in two minutes, I'll detonate it. It's your choice. I hope you make the right decision.'

Then the transmat activated again, and the Doctor faded from view.

Reginta stared at the empty space where the Doctor had been and then down at the massive bomb. For a moment he considered the possibility that the Doctor had been bluffing, but he dismissed the idea at once. The Doctor didn't seem the sort to bluff – he had meant what he said.

With a snarl of annoyance, Reginta turned to the navigator and barked orders to take the ship out of Earth's orbit and head for home immediately.

Back on Earth, the Doctor reappeared in the general's storeroom.

'You won't have any more problems with big lizards,' he assured Colonel Preston and the other soldiers. 'I think they got the message. Now, if we could all move back into the general's office for a moment?'

The Doctor ushered them all out of the storeroom and closed the door behind them. A few moments later, there was a muffled explosion as the transmat self-destructed.

'Sorry about the mess,' the Doctor said. 'But I can't leave anachronistic equipment just lying about. Now,' he went on, 'I'd best be on my way.'

Colonel Preston accompanied the Doctor back to the main gate.

'You're not really working for Eisenhower, are you?' he asked as they shook hands.

'No,' the Doctor admitted. 'I don't work for anyone.'

'Well, whoever you are,' Preston said, 'thank you.'

The Doctor smiled. 'My pleasure,' he said. 'Now, you go and win the war.'

'That's the plan,' Colonel Preston said.

'I may not work for him,' the Doctor said, 'but Eisenhower knows what he's doing.' Then he turned and walked out of the base, heading back towards the TARDIS.

Your story starts here . . .

Do you **love books** and
discovering new stories?
Then **www.puffin.co.uk**
is the place for you . . .

• Thrilling adventures, fantastic fiction
and laugh-out-loud fun

• Brilliant videos featuring your favourite authors
and characters

• Exciting competitions, news, activities,
the Puffin blog and SO MUCH more . . .

www.puffin.co.uk

 **Listen**

Do you love listening to stories?

Want to know what happens behind the scenes in a recording studio?

Hear funny sound effects, exclusive author interviews and the best books read by famous authors and actors on the **Puffin Podcast** at **www.puffin.co.uk**

#ListenWithPuffin